THE SOLUTION OF A MYSTERY

THE SOLUTION OF A MYSTERY

DOCUMENTS RELATIVE TO THE MURDER OF ROGER MAIDMENT AT ULLATHWAITE IN THE COUNTY OF YORKSHIRE IN OCTOBER 1899, COLLECTED BY PHILIP WYNYARD WRENNE, M.A., J.P., D.L., AND EDITED BY

J. S. FLETCHER

BROWNSTONE BOOKS

First published in 1932.

INTRODUCTION

Joseph Smith Fletcher (1863–1935) was an English journalist and author. He wrote more than 230 books on a wide variety of subjects, both fiction and non-fiction, and was one of the most prolific English writers of detective fiction—the work for which he is chiefly remembered today.

Fletcher was born in Halifax, West Yorkshire, the son of a clergyman. His father died when he was eight months old, and his grandmother took him in and raised him on a farm in Darrington, near Pontefract, in Yorkshire. He was educated at Silcoates School in Wakefield, and after some study of law, became a journalist at age 20.

He started work as a sub-editor in London, but soon returned to Yorkshire, where he worked first on the Leeds *Mercury* using the pseudonym "A Son of the Soil," and then as a special correspondent for the *Yorkshire Post*. Among other things, he covered Edward VII's coronation in 1902.

Fletcher's first books published were poetry. He then wrote numerous, and now largely forgotten, works of historical fiction and history, many dealing with Yorkshire. His regional work led to his selection as a fellow of the Royal Historical Society.

Michael Sadleir stated that Fletcher's historical novel, *When Charles I Was King* (1892), was his best work. Fletcher wrote several novels of rural life in imitation of Richard Jefferies, beginning with *The Wonderful Wapentake* (1894), but it wasn't until 1914, when Fletcher wrote his first detective novel, that he truly found his calling.

Over the last two decates of his life, he went on to write over a hundred more mysteries, many featuring the private investigator Ronald Camberwell.

Fletcher is sometimes incorrectly described as a "Golden Age of Detective Fiction" author, but he is in fact an almost exact contemporary of Arthur Conan Doyle, the creator of Sherlock Holmes. The bulk of his detective fiction works considerably pre-date the period considered the Golden Age, and even those few published within it do not conform to the closed form and strict rules professed, if not unfailingly observed, by Golden Age writers.

His work is still enjoyable today. Although some volumes have mildly racist elements, as were common in fiction of the era, the modern reader should keep in mind the period in which they were originally published.

—Karl Wurf
Rockville, Maryland

PREFATORY NOTE BY THE EDITOR

There recently died, at his country seat, Wrenne Park, near Ullathwaite, in Yorkshire, Mr Philip Wynyard Wrenne, a gentleman greatly respected in the county for his character, his abilities, and his devotion to the public service. Mr Wrenne—as an eighteenth-century writer would have said—was a man of parts. Born into the world of a good old family, endowed from childhood with more than ample means, educated at Eton and at King's College, Cambridge, where he proceeded to his master's degree at an unusually early age, he entered upon life with every advantage. He was a sound classical scholar and edited and translated a well-known edition of Horace. His real bent, however, was towards archæology and antiquarianism: a great collector of old books and old furniture, he left behind him one of the finest private libraries in England and a gathering of Elizabethan and Caroline chairs, tables, and presses which probably has never been equalled in variety and value. But he had other interests. Placed on the Commission of the Peace while still a young man, he became a model and indefatigable magistrate, and for over thirty years presided over the local bench, and for half that time was chairman of Quarter Sessions. He also filled other important public offices in the county, of which he was a Deputy Lieutenant.

During Mr Wrenne's time as chairman of the Ullathwaite magistrates an extraordinary case of murder occurred in the town. A man named Roger Maidment, employed as a collector of rents, was mysteriously murdered and robbed one night when returning from his collecting round. Suspicion fell on a young man of a somewhat wild character, Richard Radford, whose father, a highly respectable solicitor, was at the time Mayor of Ullathwaite. Richard Radford was arrested, and after various appearances before the local bench was duly committed to the Grandminster Assizes for trial. In due course he was tried, and, though the circumstantial evidence against him was undoubtedly strong, he was acquitted, and the mystery of Maidment's murder remained unsolved. It was felt by every one in the neighbourhood that the truth in this matter had never been approached, and no one was more inquisitive about it than Mr Wrenne.

Some time after the trial Mr Wrenne privately induced three people to set down in writing their impressions of the case and to deposit their statements with him. One of these persons was the Superintendent of Police at Ullathwaite. Another was the solicitor for the defence. The third was the foreman of the jury which acquitted Richard Radford. And some years later, when all the principal persons concerned were dead, Mr Wrenne persuaded Richard Radford himself to complete the *dossier* by writing his story—in which lay the solution of the mystery.

On the death of Mr Wrenne these four manuscripts, duly authenticated and sealed, were found among his papers, and, in consequence of a direction in his will, were handed over to me by his executors, with instructions to make them public. As Richard Radford, like all the other actors in the drama, is now dead, and the telling of the truth as regards the murder of Roger Maidment can do no harm to anyone, these accounts of what happened, written from four different standpoints, may now be given to the world.

J. S. FLETCHER

Falklands, Dorking

MEMORANDUM BY MR WRENNE

Prefixed to the four authenticated documents referred to in the foregoing editorial note.

The four papers herein enclosed, relative to the murder of Roger Maidment, at Ullathwaite, in October 1899, were obtained by me on the following dates:

1. Statement of Charles Henderson, Superintendent of Police at Ullathwaite	*July 1900*
2. Statement of Ernest Henry Wilsborough, Solicitor, of Ullathwaite	*Aug. 1900*
3. Statement of Septimus Nettleton, foreman of the jury at Grandminster Assizes at the trial of Richard Radford	*Oct. 1900*
4. Statement of Richard Radford	*Jan. 1925*

I am firmly convinced, having made a close study of all the facts, that the statement of Richard Radford embodies the absolute truth as regards the murder of Roger Maidment.

P. W. WRENNE
Wrenne Park, Ullathwaite,
December 1925

I

ACCORDING TO THE PROSECUTION

(Statement of Charles Henderson, Superintendent of Police, Ullathwaite)

At the request of Mr Philip Wynyard Wrenne, chairman of the West Riding magistrates at Ullathwaite, and as Superintendent of the West Riding Constabulary in that district, I proceed to write out, to the best of my ability, all that I know as regards the arrest and trial of Richard Radford, charged with the murder of Roger Maidment at Hagsdene Wood, on the outskirts of Ullathwaite, on the night of October 17, 1899. I shall endeavour to suppress any personal opinion of my own as regards this matter and shall confine myself to the bare facts of the case as they were presented to me in my official capacity. And here I had better explain a certain point in order to make things clear. Ullathwaite, as a borough, has its own borough police and magistrates; they deal with crimes and offences occurring within the borough. Hagsdene Wood, however, is outside the borough boundary; hence the Maidment affair came within the jurisdiction of the county police and justices and became my duty to investigate.

Ullathwaite is a small market-town in the purely agricultural part of the West Riding of Yorkshire. Its population in 1891 was a little over 4000. Except on market, fair, and auction days it is a slow-going, sleepy place. Being so small everybody—of any consequence—is well known; I mean, everybody is, so to speak, known to everybody else. Society follows the usual lines of English division. In and round about the town there is a small percentage of the upper class. There is a larger one of the middle class, subdivided into the various sections of professional folk, clergy, doctors, lawyers, bankers, better-class tradesmen and people engaged in commerce; beneath these comes the always more numerous class of workers in one or other line of labour. It is safe to repeat, however—and it is pertinent to what I shall have to say in this statement—that in Ullathwaite, whatever his rank or class, almost every man is well known to the rest of his fellow-townsmen. Those familiar with English country-town life will know what I mean when I say that the local newspaper, the *Ullathwaite Advertiser*, prints nothing but purely local news, and that its editor would regard the production of a monster gooseberry or abnormal vegetable-marrow by John Smith, market gardener, as being of vastly more importance to his readers than an eruption of Vesuvius or a revolution in Brazil.

Being an unmarried man, I live in lodgings, instead of having a house of my own. I lodge with Mrs Marriner, at Oak Cottage, a little way outside the town, on its western border and beyond the borough boundary. I have there three excellent rooms: two sitting-rooms, one of which I use as an office, and a bedroom which has a private bathroom attached to it. About half-past seven o'clock on the morning of October 18, 1899, I was in this bathroom when Mrs Marriner's servant-maid, Esther Thorp, came knocking at the door, calling my name.

'Mr Henderson, Mr Henderson!' she cried. 'There's a man downstairs, sir, says he must see you at once!'

'Who is he?' I called. 'What name?'

'I think it's Mr Wrenne's gamekeeper, sir,' she answered. 'But I don't know his name. He says he must see you immediate!'

'Tell him I'll be there in five minutes,' I said.

I got out of my bath, had a rub down, and got into some clothes and a dressing-gown. I knew Mr Wrenne's gamekeeper well enough, a man named Sevidge, and I guessed that if, or as, he wanted me there had been some scrap between him and poachers during the night. But when I went downstairs and saw him standing in Mrs Marriner's kitchen I knew that there was something more serious than that.

'What is it, Sevidge?' I asked.

He glanced round to make sure that we were alone. Then he came close.

'It's murder, Mr Henderson!' he said in a low voice. 'Do you know that young fellow Maidment—Roger Maidment?'

'The rent-collector?' I replied. 'Yes!'

'He's lying there in Hagsdene Wood—dead,' he went on. 'I found him just now, as I was on my way to Wrenne Park. Been lying there all night from the look of him—clothes wet through, and so on.'

'What makes you think it's murder?' I asked.

'Ah!' he answered. 'No doubt of it. There's a wound on his left temple—but you'll see for yourself. And—his pockets are all turned inside out. Murdered—and robbed!'

'Anybody else know?' I inquired.

'Not that I'm aware of,' he replied. 'I found him by accident—and came straight back to you.'

'Very well,' I said. 'Now do something for me, Sevidge. The nearest of my men is Walshaw——'

'I know where he lives,' he said.

'Run down to him, then,' I continued. 'Tell him to get two or three other men and to see Dr Simpson, and bring them all as quickly as possible to Hagsdene Wood. Then come back here and I'll go along with you.'

He was an obliging fellow, Sevidge, and he hastened away there and then, while I hurried upstairs to finish dressing. While I dressed, I reflected on what I knew of Roger Maidment. He was a young fellow of, perhaps, five-and-twenty years of age, who, having been a clerk in an accountant's office, had recently set up for himself as a collector of rents, and, I believe, had got quite a nice little business together. I happened to know, too, that he collected the rents of some property that lay on the farther side of Hagsdene Wood; probably he had been returning with the money in his pocket when, as Sevidge seemed to suggest, he had been waylaid, murdered, and robbed.

Sevidge was back within half an hour; as soon as I had swallowed a cup of tea and a mouthful of bread I set out with him. Hagsdene Wood was half a mile away. It was a bit of old woodland, thick with ancient oak and beech, which lay between the outskirts of the town and Wrenne Park—a gloomy and lonely place, intersected by two or three paths which formed short cuts from the neighbouring roads and lanes. And it was within a few yards of one of these paths that I found Maidment's dead body: it had evidently been dragged from the path to where it lay. One glance at the dead man's face and head showed me what had happened. He had been struck a terrible blow on the left temple—a blow sufficient to cause death, and probably repeated. Another glance confirmed what Sevidge had already told me—the dead man's pockets had been turned out.

There was nothing to be done till my men and the doctor arrived, and as I was not very familiar with Hagsdene Wood I looked round to get my bearings. Through the trees, perhaps fifty or sixty yards away, at the edge of the wood, I saw the roof and chimneys of a house: it appeared to be the only house anywhere near where we stood.

'Whose house is that, Sevidge?' I asked. 'I suppose you know?'

'Yes, sir,' he answered. 'Mr Hebb lives there.'

I knew all about Hebb. He was managing clerk to Mr John Radford, a well-known solicitor of the town, and at that time Mayor of Ullathwaite.

'I'll just step across and find out if they heard anything during the night,' I said. 'If Dr Simpson and the police come while I'm away, tell them I'll be back in a few minutes. Touch nothing, Sevidge, till they come.'

'No intention, sir!' he replied grimly. 'Not to my taste.'

I went across the wood to Hebb's house. It was a small place, an old-fashioned cottage really, standing in a pretty, tree-surrounded garden. I knocked at the front door, which faced the edge of the wood—knocked twice before I got any response. Then I heard a key turned, a bolt drawn; the door opened, and I found myself confronting Mrs Hebb. She was a very pretty, well-developed young woman of perhaps twenty-five years of age, the English type of fair hair and blue eyes; an attractive woman altogether. That I had disturbed her before she could complete her toilet was evident; her hair was loose about her shoulders, and she was still in a dressing-gown. Her eyes opened wide when she saw me—I was, of course, well known to her by sight, though I could not remember seeing her before.

'Good morning, Mrs Hebb,' I said. 'Sorry to disturb you. But—something's happened just inside the wood there, and I wanted to ask you if you or your husband heard any sounds of a struggle or anything of that sort last evening, or during the night?'

Mrs Hebb turned very pale—indeed, the colour completely left her cheeks, which were naturally very rosy.

'Last night?' she faltered. 'I—we—I—we never——'

Hebb suddenly appeared behind his wife—in his shirt and trousers. He too stared at the sight of me.

'Something wrong, Superintendent?' he asked.

'There's something very wrong,' I replied. 'I don't want to alarm Mrs Hebb, though. I came to ask if you or she, or both, heard any sound—cries, anything of that sort—from this wood last evening, or during the night?'

Hebb shook his head.

'I was out till nearly midnight last night,' he answered. 'It was my night at the School Board meeting at Heckinley—I'm clerk there, you know. I don't get back till the very last train. No. I heard nothing during the night. Did you, Lettie?'

'I heard nothing,' replied Mrs Hebb. Her colour was coming back, and her voice grew firm. 'Neither last evening nor during the night.'

'What is it, Superintendent?' asked Hebb. 'Poachers?'

'The fact is,' I answered, 'there's a dead man lying in the wood. You know him, I dare say. Maidment—Roger Maidment, the rent-collector.'

I was watching them both narrowly as I said this. Mrs Hebb's pretty face puckered itself into a look of something like fear; Hebb simply stared.

'Good Lord!' he exclaimed. 'Maidment! Ah!—last night, I happen to know, was the night he collected rents from that property the other side of Hagsdene Wood. He used to make a short cut across the wood coming back—I've met him now and then. But—do you say he's dead?'

'Murdered!' I answered. 'And robbed, too, no doubt. Well, you heard nothing?'

'Nothing!' they said, speaking together. 'Nothing at all.'

I left them and went back to the wood. My men had just arrived with Dr Simpson: we stood by while the doctor made a preliminary examination of the dead man.

'He's been struck two heavy blows with some blunt weapon—perhaps a very heavy walking-stick,' he said, rising from his knees. 'Either would be sufficient to kill.' Then, glancing at the turned-out pockets, he added, 'Case of murder for the sake of robbery, I suppose?'

'How long do you think he's been dead, doctor?' I asked. 'We must fix the approximate time if we can.'

Dr Simpson looked at his watch.

'It's now nearly half-past eight,' he replied. 'I should say he's been dead—and death would be instantaneous—roughly speaking, about ten hours.'

'That would make it about half-past ten last night,' I remarked.

'About,' he assented.

Having given certain orders to my men about the removal of the body, and the fencing off and guarding of the place where it had been found, I took Sevidge with me and, leaving Hagsdene Wood by the opposite side, went to visit the tenants of the property between it and Wrenne Park from whom Maidment collected rents.

2

The houses to which Sevidge and I now repaired made a little colony of their own, set in a narrow valley on the western side of Hagsdene Wood, and near the main entrance to Wrenne Park. I knew something about them and their owner. A few years previously a retired tradesman of Ullathwaite, Mr Stephen Winterbotham, having the chance of securing it at a fairly low price, had bought up the land in this valley, and had thereupon caused to be built some twelve or fifteen residences of the small villa type. Once erected, they had let readily, and were now all in occupancy. Mr Winterbotham, having amused and occupied himself by watching their construction, had, as soon as they were all finished and let, retired to enjoy the rest of his life at Scarborough, and had entrusted the collection of his rents to Roger Maidment. And Maidment, as I quickly ascertained, always called in person for the rents on the 17th day of each month. Why on that particular date I do not know, unless it was that the leases or agreements dated from some previous 17th.

I had no difficulty in getting the information I wanted. Maidment had been there the night before, and, going from house to house, had duly collected his rents. Some of the tenants had paid him by cheque; some in banknotes; some in gold; the total amount he received came to something like £112. More than a half of this was in notes and gold. Whether he had other moneys on him in addition to this when he was attacked, murdered, and robbed it was not, of course, possible to say: perhaps he had.

Nor had I any difficulty in ascertaining particulars about a highly important matter in reconstructing Maidment's doings—the matter of exact time. Maidment had made his first call at the houses in Hagsdene Park—the general name of the little colony—at a quarter to nine the previous evening; his last at ten o'clock. He had stayed chatting a little at the last place; it would, they said, be about a quarter past ten when he left. As far as Sevidge and I could reckon things it would take him about twenty minutes to walk from this house to where his dead body was found in Hagsdene Wood.

Sevidge and I were coming away with this information—I had made a note of the various amounts collected by Maidment, and of the times concerned—when I heard my name called from one of the houses, and turned to find a tenant named Collingwood hailing me from his window.

'Will you come back a minute, Superintendent?' he called. 'I've something to tell you.'

We went back; Collingwood met us at his door and took us into his parlour. I had, of course, told him, as I had told all the other tenants, of what had happened.

'I've just thought of something that may be of use to you,' he said. 'It's a small matter, but I suppose it's in these cases as in most others—every little helps. As I told you before, I paid Maidment my month's rent, six pounds, last night in gold—six sovereigns. Now amongst the six there was a sovereign with a hole in it!'

'A hole?' I exclaimed.

'A small hole—just drilled through, under the rim,' he answered. 'As if it had been used as a pendant on a watch-chain. I don't know where I got it—in change, somewhere, I suppose. I'd never noticed it, never known that I had it until I was counting out the six sovereigns to Maidment. Then we both noticed it. He made some remark about defaced coinage. I offered to go upstairs and get him another. No, he said, it wasn't worth the trouble: he'd shove it into the bank amongst all the others; he said they'd never notice it. But—there it is! A sovereign with a hole in it. Worth anything as a clue, Superintendent?'

It was a very small clue, but, after all, it was a clue, and I made a note of it. A sovereign . . . through which a small hole had been drilled.

3

I went back to my rooms at Mrs Marriner's after this, to get my breakfast and to think things over before going into the town. It seemed to me that certain things were obvious. Maidment had been murdered for the money he had on him. Could the murderer be traced through that money? Now I had made particular inquiries among the tenants at Hagsdene Park as to how they paid their rents the previous evening—I mean, in what form. As I have already said, some had paid by cheque, some in notes, some in gold. Well, as to the cheques, the murderer would certainly destroy them as being of no use to him. As to the banknotes, it would be difficult to trace them, for of all the people who had paid Maidment in that way not a single one had taken the precaution to note down the numbers of the notes with which they had parted. As to the gold, how could any man distinguish one coin and another? But . . . there was the sovereign through which a hole had been drilled. If we could trace that . . .

It is unnecessary to enter into the details of the work we did that morning in our efforts to come across some trace of the murderer. I set all my men to work, of course—uniformed and plain-clothes men. A thorough examination of the surroundings of the scene of the murder was made—we got some impressions of footprints, but they were so many and varied (for the paths through that wood were a good deal used) that I felt them to be of no value. Investigation showed nothing unusual in Maidment's doings the day of his death. He had been at his office or about the town all day; he had gone to his lodgings—he was a single man, and not a native of Ullathwaite—at the end of the afternoon, and after having his usual tea-supper, or high tea, had set off for Hagsdene Park. All this was unilluminative. Inquiries among the lodging-houses and at the casual ward of the workhouse failed to reveal the presence in the town of any undesirable or suspicious characters. And at noon I was still without any direct clue as to the identity of the murderer.

Then came a startling revelation. Just before one o'clock, when, after a strenuous morning's work, I was about leaving my office for lunch at the Black Bull, Ullathwaite's principal hotel, Collingwood, the man whom I had seen at Hagsdene Park earlier in the day and who had told me about the debased sovereign, called, bringing with him a man whom I knew by sight as one Fardale, a bookmaker. There was an air of mystery, mingled with concern, about both which I was quick to perceive.

'Can we have a word or two with you—in private—Mr Superintendent?' asked Collingwood. 'It's—about this morning's affair.'

I took them into my private room and closed the door. Even then Collingwood dropped his voice to something like a whisper, as men do when they want to be very confidential.

'You know Mr Fardale?' he began. 'Know who and what he is, anyway. Mr Fardale's a friend of mine. We often meet at the Black Bull—met there just now. Of course, we've been talking about the murder. Everybody's talking about it. I told Mr Fardale about paying my month's rent to Maidment last night, and about that sovereign that I told you of this morning; the sovereign with a hole drilled through it.'

'Yes?' I said, wondering what was to come. 'Yes?'

Collingwood turned in his chair, nodding at Fardale, who so far had sat staring stolidly at me.

'He's got it!' he said. 'Fardale!'

I turned to Fardale. Without a word he plunged a hand into his right-hand hip-pocket and, drawing out a quantity of gold coins, picked out one and passed it to me. There it was—a sovereign of the reign of Queen Victoria, with a small hole drilled through it just under the rim, above the head of the figure. I held it out to Collingwood.

'Are you sure that's the coin you spoke to me of as having paid to Maidment last night?' I asked. 'Dead sure?'

'I'm so sure, Mr Superintendent, that I'm willing to take my oath on it!' he answered with emphasis. 'It is the coin!'

Once more I turned to Fardale.

'Where did you get this coin, Mr Fardale?' I asked. 'You'll tell me, of course?'

Fardale shifted uneasily in his chair. He was evidently much disturbed.

'I'm in a very difficult position, Mr Superintendent,' he said. 'A very unpleasant position! You know what I am—a bookmaker. Well, I've my clients to consider. I've clients in this town and neighbourhood whose identity you'd never suspect—they'd never come to me again if they thought I let their names out. You understand, sir?'

'I understand quite well, Mr Fardale,' I replied. 'But—this is a case of murder.'

'Aye, I know that!' he assented. 'If it hadn't been, I'd never have told Collingwood what I did, nor come here with him. Well!—I suppose I must speak. I've had that coin, Mr Superintendent, since half-past ten this morning. It was paid to me by young Radford—Dick Radford!'

For the life I could not repress an exclamation.

'Good God!' I said. 'The Mayor's son?'

'That's it!' he answered. 'The Mayor's son. Only son.'

I had been standing until then: now I sat down at my desk.

'You'll explain matters, Mr Fardale?' I said. 'You see how serious this is?'

'I know,' he replied. 'Yes, I'll tell all I can, now. This lad has been betting with me—and no doubt with others—for a year or more. He's a bit shifty. When he wins he wants his money there and then, but when he loses he's not so keen about putting accounts straight. And lately he's been owing me about fifty pounds. I've had to dun him for it. Last week I just got sick of him, and I gave him an ultimatum. I told him that if he didn't pay me my fifty pounds by eleven o'clock to-day (I was giving him a full week in which to raise it) I should tell his father about the affair and refuse all further business with him himself. And I let him see that I meant what I said!'

'Well?' I asked as he paused. 'And——'

'And at half-past ten this morning he came to me,' continued Fardale. 'He handed me the fifty pounds. Forty-five pounds of it was in five-pound notes—nine of 'em. I've got 'em here. Six pounds was in gold—the precise amount owing was fifty-one pounds. Now, to assure you on the point, I put the banknotes in this pocket—left-hand hip—and the gold in this—right-hand hip. That fifty-one pounds is the only money I've received from anybody this morning. As soon as Collingwood told me, at the Black Bull, about the marked sovereign, I pulled out the six pounds in gold which Dick Radford had given me and examined each coin. I found the sovereign you've now got in your hand. And—that's all I know. I'm sorry to have to tell all this—but, as you say, it's murder!'

I sat for a moment in silence, staring at the coin. I was thinking. I knew Dick Radford as a rather rackety, wild young fellow, but I should never have thought him capable of murder.

'You'll leave this marked sovereign with me, Mr Fardale?' I said at last. 'You perceive its importance?'

'I'll do more than that, sir,' he answered, drawing out banknotes from one pocket and gold from the other. 'I'll hand all this over to you. That's the exact amount, and in the identical notes and coins, that Dick Radford handed to me. And . . . what'll come next, Mr Superintendent?'

But to that question I made no answer, and the two men went away.

4

I was in no mood for going to the Black Bull for lunch after that, and, sending out for some bread, cheese, and ale, I sat down to think matters over. In any case, I foresaw a terrible catastrophe for Mr Radford senior, at that time just completing his term of office as Mayor of Ullathwaite, and, as I knew, about to be re-elected for another year. Mr Radford was the leading solicitor of the town—a man of about fifty years of age, a quiet, reserved, eminently respectable (and highly respected) gentleman, who from, I believe, quite humble beginnings had built up a considerable practice. In addition to being Mayor—he had long been on the Town Council as councillor or alderman—he filled various other important posts in the town, and was a county as well as a borough magistrate. He was well-to-do, also; probably quite a wealthy man; early in life, when he was beginning to get on, he had married the daughter of a leading tradesman in Birmingham, a well-educated young woman who at one time had been engaged in teaching, and it was said that she had brought him a very handsome fortune. Mr and Mrs Radford were a sort of model pair;

they lived in a beautiful house, of which they were very proud; entertained a good deal, and were popular. They had two children: a girl, Audrey, now aged twenty-one; a boy, Richard, now a year younger. Audrey, educated at Cheltenham and in Paris, was something of a highbrow young lady and was deeply interested in various intellectual movements. But Dick, it was well known, was something of a throw-back. Articled to his father, it was matter of common knowledge that he found it difficult to pass any legal examination; moreover, neither his father nor his mother appeared to be able to exercise any control over him. Without being actually bad or vicious, in the worst sense of the term, he was wild, irresponsible, weak, with tastes for horses, dogs, cards, billiards, and low company. But . . . murder? I could scarcely bring myself to believe him capable of that. Still . . . there was Fardale's evidence. And it might be that if he did attack Maidment in order to rob him and so put himself in funds he only meant to stun him while he emptied his pockets. But that, of course, would amount to murder. Anyhow, I saw that I should have to see Dick Radford's father. Him first; then Dick. And the prospect of seeing the Mayor was by no means pleasant. I determined, however, to get it over at once.

But before I could step across to the Town Hall, where I knew Mr Radford could be found about that time, I had two more visitors. These were shown in to me just as I was finishing my improvised lunch, a young man and a young woman, he of the artisan, she of the servant-maid class. The young man was shy and diffident; the girl seemed confident and assured.

'Well,' I said, when I had bidden them be seated. 'What do you want to see me about?'

The two exchanged glances. It was evident that each wanted the other to begin. But it was the girl who spoke first.

'It's about what happened in Hagsdene Wood last night, sir,' she said. 'We—you see, we know something.'

'Oh, you do, do you?' I said. 'Well, to begin with, who are you? Give me your names and occupations.'

'My name's Ellen Hopkinson, sir,' replied the girl readily. 'I'm parlourmaid at Mrs Rivers's, Hagsdene Park. This is my young man, James Collier—he's a plumber, at Mr Walker's. Why don't you speak for yourself, Jim?'

'You're speaking!' retorted Jim, with a sheepish grin. 'One'll do!'

I jotted down the names and looked at the girl.

'Well, Ellen?' I said. 'What is it?'

Ellen looked at Jim.

'Which is to tell?' she asked.

'Go on!' he answered. 'You're readiest at talking. I'm listening.'

'Well, sir,' Ellen continued, turning to me. 'It's like this. Last night was my night out. I came into town; Jim met me, and we went to his mother's to supper—that was after we'd had a walk round. Then Jim saw me home. We went through Hagsdene Wood. We stopped a bit by a gate there, talking—it was a bit before my time for going in—and while we were there we saw something that we thought was strange—somebody, that is, that was what you'd call behaving strange.'

'Yes?' I said. 'Who?'

Ellen looked at Jim; Jim looked at the ceiling.

'I suppose it's all between ourselves, sir?' inquired Ellen.

'Absolutely—at present,' I answered. 'This is confidential.'

'Well, sir, it was young Mr Dick Radford!' she said. 'Just him!'

'You know him well by sight?' I asked.

'Ought to!' she retorted. 'I lived there, at Mr Radford's, for two years. I know Mr Dick well enough!'

'Well—go on, then,' I said. 'What did you see last night?'

'Well, sir, we saw this,' she continued. 'There's a narrow lane runs on the far side of the wood; me and Jim were leaning against a gate there, a gate that opens into the wood. We saw somebody coming along the lane on a bicycle; saw the lamp, some distance off. So—we opened the gate and slipped into the wood, behind the hedge.'

'Why?' I asked, inconsequently.

'Don't know, sir—we did, anyway,' she answered. 'Then the man on the bicycle came up to the gate and got off. He bent over his lamp for a minute; it was then we saw his face and saw who it was—young Mr Dick Radford. He——'

'Stay a moment,' I interrupted. I turned to Jim. 'Did you see him?'

'I did, sir!' replied Jim firmly. 'She's right!'

'You know him well by sight?'

'I do, sir. Ever since he was that height.'

I turned and nodded to Ellen. She went on with her story.

'He turned out his lamp, sir,' she said. 'Then he opened the gate and wheeled the bicycle into the wood. We could just make out that he pushed it between the hedge that separates the wood from the lanes and some bushes that grow just inside. Then he lit a cigarette: we saw his face again, quite clearly. And then he went off into the wood; we heard him for a minute or two.'

'In which direction?' I asked.

She hesitated a moment; then she seemed to think of something.

'Do you know where Mr Hebb lives, sir—the other side of the wood from where we were?' she asked. 'Well, he went that way.'

'You say you heard him for a minute or two? Did things become quiet then?'

'Yes, sir, perfectly quiet.'

'What did you two do?'

'Nipped out of the gate and went on, sir.'

'To Hagsdene Park?'

'Yes, sir—to Mrs Rivers's.'

'What time was it when you saw Mr Dick Radford?'

'It would be all about ten o'clock, sir. My time for going in is half-past.'

'It was ten o'clock,' remarked Jim stolidly. 'I heard the town clock.'

'Did you meet anyone between Hagsdene Wood and Hagsdene Park?'

'No, sir!'

'Not Mr Maidment?'

'We never met anybody, sir.'

'Did you see or hear anything or anybody as you came back after leaving Ellen, Collier?' I inquired.

'Neither heard nor saw anything, sir! I didn't come back by the wood; I came round by the road,' replied Jim.

I thought a bit.

'Have you mentioned all this to anybody?' I asked.

'Only to Mrs Rivers, sir. She said to get Jim at once and come to you,' replied Ellen. 'Which, of course, we've done. Jim not being very willing, though, sir.'

'Don't like shoving my nose into other people's affairs,' grunted Jim. 'Not my business, after all. But you would have me come!'

'All right, my lad,' I said. 'No harm done. Now go away—and just keep all this to yourselves for the time being. And you, Ellen, tell your mistress to keep quiet about it. Understand?'

'I understand, sir,' said Ellen. 'But she's a very reserved lady, Mrs Rivers; she won't talk, and I shan't, and Jim—well, you can see for yourself, sir, he's not a very great hand with his tongue, at any time.'

'Very excellent characteristic!' I said. 'Very well—keep quiet till you hear more from me.'

They went away—Ellen evidently needlessly admonishing Jim to utter silence—and once more I turned to the inevitable. I must see Dick Radford's father—and at once.

5

I went to this interview with Mr Radford feeling more uncomfortable than I had ever felt in all my previous experience of uncomfortable things—and that, in my walk of life, is saying a good deal. I knew the Mayor for a hard-working, sober, serious man; a model husband and father, as far as I knew; certainly a model citizen. And I knew that though there was little doubt that he had already had a good deal to trouble him in relation to his only son, the suggestion that that son had had something to do with the murder and robbery of Maidment would be terrible in the extreme. Moreover, there was the lad's mother to think of—and his sister. Still, it had got to be done.

I found Mr Radford in the Mayor's Parlour. He had been very busy all that day, his clerk told me while I waited to see him, and he himself looked at me with some show of impatience when I entered.

'Can't give you very long, Henderson,' he said, motioning me to a chair by his desk. 'Several important committees this afternoon. What can I do for you?'

I went straight to the point.

'Mr Mayor,' I said, 'you have, of course, heard of the murder of Maidment, the rent-collector, which, we believe, occurred last night in Hagsdene Wood?'

'Heard of it, yes,' he answered. 'But that's outside the borough—it's in your sphere. The borough police don't come in.'

'Just so, Mr Mayor,' I agreed. 'But that's not quite the question. What we are concerned about—borough as well as county police—is who is the murderer. That, of course, is *the* question!'

He looked at me narrowly.

'Any clue—any idea—any information?' he asked sharply.

'Yes!' I said. 'I'm sorry to say.'

'Why sorry?' he interrupted.

'That will appear,' I answered. 'But may I explain matters? Maidment had gone to Hagsdene Park last night to collect the rents there. He collected them. I have investigated the circumstances of all the payments. One tenant, Mr Collingwood, paid Maidment his month's rent, six pounds, in gold. Amongst the six sovereigns which he handed to Maidment there was one which was marked.'

'Marked!' he exclaimed. 'A marked sovereign?'

'A sovereign, Mr Mayor, which had a small hole drilled through it,' I replied. 'A very small hole, such as would take the link of a thin watch-chain. But—there it was!'

'Is Collingwood certain of that?' he asked.

'Absolutely certain!' I answered.

'He'd swear to it?'

'He would swear to it!'

Mr Radford got up and walked about the room: he appeared to be thinking hard. Suddenly he faced round on me.

'What about the rest of the money collected by Maidment?' he asked. 'I know something about that property. He'd probably collect a hundred pounds or so last night.'

'About a hundred and twelve pounds, Mr Mayor,' I replied. 'I reckoned it all up, from the information given me by the tenants.'

'He was robbed of it, of course,' he went on. 'Any trace of it?'

'A certain amount was in the form of cheques,' I said. 'Some of it was paid in banknotes. As regards the gold, I may as well come to the point. I have traced the perforated sovereign.'

He was still walking about the room, still, evidently, deep in thought, but at that he wheeled quickly round and stood staring at me as if incredulous.

'You've—traced—the perforated sovereign?' he exclaimed. 'Already!'

'Already, Mr Mayor—though not by any work on the part of me or my men,' I replied. 'Accidentally! The sovereign in question was paid to Fardale, the bookmaker, at half-past ten this morning. It is now in my possession.'

He stopped from his pacing up and down and, standing on the hearthrug before his fire, looked hard at me. It seemed a long time before he spoke—and though I am no weakling I could hear my heart thumping like a sledge-hammer.

'Who paid it to Fardale?' he asked at length. 'Who?'

I drew a long breath.

'Mr Mayor,' I said, 'this is the most painful thing I have ever had to do in the whole course of my experience. But I'm obliged to do it. Mr Mayor, the marked sovereign was paid to Fardale by your son!'

I was scarcely prepared for what followed. Mr Radford was a man of sallow, almost dark, complexion; he was also, as far as I had known him, of calm, composed temperament. But now his face turned white, white to the lips; his lips drew back, showing his teeth: I saw his hands move and his fingers stretch themselves out like the claws of some bird of prey; for an instant I thought he was going to spring at me. Then his voice came, hoarsely.

'That's a lie—a damned lie!' he snarled. 'A lie!'

'No, sir!' I said. 'It's the truth. Fardale is an honest man—and Collingwood has identified the coin. There is no doubt of the truth of what I have told you, Mr Mayor; your son paid the marked sovereign to Fardale this morning.'

'Why should my son pay money to Fardale?' he demanded. 'A low-down bookmaker!'

'Your son, sir, has been in the habit of betting with Fardale for some time,' I replied. 'He owed Fardale fifty-one pounds. Last week Fardale told him that unless he paid the full amount by eleven o'clock this morning, the 18th, he should tell you of the matter and should refuse to do any further business with him. This morning, at half-past ten, your son called on Fardale and paid the money in notes and gold. I have them both—gold and notes—just as Fardale received them.'

'Why did Fardale come to you?' he demanded. 'How did he know——?'

'Fardale met Collingwood at the Black Bull, Mr Mayor—they are friends,' I replied. 'Collingwood told him of the marked sovereign. Fardale immediately remembered your son's payment, and that the money given him lay in a certain pocket, untouched—it was the only money he had received this morning. He at once examined the gold and found the sovereign in question. Collingwood identified it there and then. So—they came to me, as they were bound to do.'

He was once more walking up and down, thinking, I could see, harder than ever.

Suddenly he again twisted round on me and clapped his hands together.

'Come to the point!' he said. 'Are you accusing my son, Richard Radford, of the murder and robbery of this fellow? Speak out!'

'I shall have to ask Mr Richard to explain his possession of the marked sovereign, Mr Mayor,' I replied.

'I'll soon knock whatever theories you've got on the head!' he retorted angrily. 'If my son had murdered and robbed Maidment he'd have had to be here—that is to say, in Hagsdene Wood—last night. Well, I, as his father, happen to know he wasn't, and couldn't have been. My son wasn't within thirty miles of Ullathwaite last night, from six o'clock onward, till breakfast—or, rather, office time this morning. So there you are!' he concluded triumphantly. 'Alibi, eh?—case of alibi!'

'Where was your son, Mr Mayor?' I asked quietly.

'Well, I can tell you that, too!' he said, defiantly. 'I'm under no obligation to, but I will. My son, as his mother and sister can tell you, left home yesterday evening at six o'clock, to visit and spend the night at his friend Mr Verrill's at Lowsthorpe. And Lowsthorpe's thirty-three miles from Ullathwaite. He went off there on his bicycle, and he didn't come back until just before ten o'clock this morning, when he went straight to the office. He was there when I reached the office at ten o'clock.'

'Do you know if he went out at half-past ten, Mr Mayor?' I inquired.

'Can't say—I went out myself, to come here, at a quarter past,' he answered. 'But at any rate he wasn't in Ullathwaite last night.'

I waited a moment. Then I got up.

'Mr Mayor,' I said, 'I may as well tell you more. Your son *was* in Ullathwaite last night! He was in Hagsdene Wood at ten o'clock. And Maidment, according to the doctors, was probably killed about half-past ten. This is the truth!'

His face went white again as he faced me.

'In Hagsdene Wood? At ten o'clock—last night?' he said. 'Who—who says so?'

'Two credible witnesses, who know him well,' I answered. 'He came there with his bicycle, hid it between the outer hedgerow and some shrubs, and then walked into the wood in the direction of Hebb's cottage.'

'Of Hebb's cottage?' he repeated. 'At—ten o'clock?'

'About ten o'clock, Mr Mayor,' I assented. 'Maidment's body was found within a short distance of Hebb's garden.'

He stared at me in silence for a minute or two.

'No!' he said. 'It's a lie! He was at Verrill's, at Lowsthorpe.'

I looked round. There was a telephone on the Mayor's desk, and a telephone directory lying close by.

'Mr Mayor,' I said, 'we will soon settle that point. If your son was at Lowsthorpe from, say, eight o'clock last night until, say, eight this morning, he certainly couldn't be in Ullathwaite! May I use your telephone a moment? Is Mr Verrill on the telephone?'

'I happen to know that he is,' he replied. 'You can use it.'

I turned up Verrill's number—he was a gentleman-farmer at Lowsthorpe—and rang him up. And in a few minutes I put back the receiver and turned to Mr Radford.

'Mr Mayor,' I said, 'Mr Verrill replies that so far from your son visiting him last night, he has not even seen him for two months!'

Once more he turned deadly pale—and this time he made no answer. I went on—I felt that the time had come for plain speaking.

'Even if your son had been at Mr Verrill's last night,' I said, 'I should want to hear his explanation of his possession of the marked sovereign. Now, Mr Mayor, I must see Mr Richard Radford at once! Where is he?'

He stood for a while, again staring and staring. Then he suddenly moved across to his desk and picked up the transmitter.

'Is Mr Richard in the office?' he asked. 'Yes? Tell him to come across to me—at the Mayor's Parlour—at once.'

6

Silence fell on that room. Mr Radford continued to pace up and down; I remained sitting in the chair at the side of his desk. It was some little time before the silence was broken. He broke it . . . at last.

'What are you going to do?' he asked abruptly.

'I can't say anything, Mr Mayor, until I have seen and questioned your son,' I replied. 'It depends upon his answers—and attitude.'

'I want to question him first,' he said. 'You'll hear my question, and his answer. Then—you can ask him what you like. But, mind you,' he went on, speaking with vehemence, 'you're on the wrong tack, Henderson! The lad has his failings, but that he's a murderer and a thief is utterly beyond all belief. The wrong tack, I say! I suppose you think you've got a *prima facie* case, eh?'

'I don't know what I've got, Mr Mayor,' I said. 'I hope your son will be able to clear things up. If——'

But just then the door opened and Richard Radford walked in and looked inquiringly from one to the other of us. He was a well-built, good-looking lad, who appeared rather older than he was. In good humour and temper he had rather a pleasant expression, but I saw as soon as he entered that he was just then in anything but a good temper. And his first words, uttered with something very like a scowl at his father, were not encouraging.

'What do you want me for?' he demanded irritably.

Mr Radford winced—obviously. It seemed to me that he was frightened.

'To ask you a question,' he answered. 'Did you go to Lowsthorpe last night?'

Dick Radford looked at his father; then at me.

'No!' he snapped out.

'Where were you, then?'

'I shan't say! What's Henderson doing here?'

Mr Radford nodded at me.

'I'm here, Mr Richard, to ask you two or three questions,' I said, 'It'll be in your own interest to answer them. Did you pay Fardale, the bookmaker, fifty-one pounds this morning, in notes and gold?'

'Who says I did?' he demanded, angrily.

'Fardale says so. Fardale has handed the money to me.'

'Fardale's a damned sneaking cad! I did pay him fifty-one pounds.'

'Thank you! Amongst the gold which you paid him there was a marked sovereign——'

'A marked sovereign!' he exclaimed, evidently in genuine surprise. 'How marked?'

'Perforated by a small hole. Where did you get it?'

'I know nothing of it! I never saw any marked sovereign. I gave him six.'

'I know—I have them. But there it is. And that marked sovereign was certainly paid last night by Mr Collingwood, of Hagsdene Park, to Maidment, the rent-collector, who, at half-past ten last night, was murdered in Hagsdene Wood. Now, how did it come into your possession?'

He stood, silent, staring at me for a full moment. Then he shook his head and a look of sheer obstinacy came over his face.

'I shall not say! You'll not get one word out of me, Henderson—not a damned word!'

'Were you in Hagsdene Wood at ten o'clock last night?' I asked. 'Will you say?'

'I'll say! I was!'

'Why? For what purpose?'

'My business! And now not a word more! Do what you like! I see what you're after. But I didn't kill Maidment, nor rob him, either. Be damned to you!'

Then with a swift movement he was outside the room and had slammed the door on us.

7

The violent banging of that door prefaced a moment's silence; then Mr Radford turned on me and snapped out a question.

'What are you going to do?'

'It can't rest where it is, Mr Mayor,' I replied. 'It'll have to be investigated—fully. You see in what mood your son is! If he's innocent——'

'He's told you he knows nothing about either murder or robbery,' he interrupted. 'He's not a liar!'

'He didn't tell you the truth, sir, about his supposed visit to Mr Verrill,' I retorted. 'If he's absolutely innocent why doesn't he tell us where he was last night, and why he was in the wood about ten o'clock, and where he got that marked sovereign? Why——?'

'I asked you—what are you going to do?' he said. 'That's what I want to know—at present.'

'I shall have to consult my superiors, Mr Mayor,' I answered. 'I suppose I ought to arrest your son now! But—will you try to get some explanation out of him? And will you give me your word that you'll keep an eye on him until to-morrow morning?'

He looked at me for a time as if pondering over what I had said. Then he began to walk up and down the room again. Several minutes passed; he seemed to be thinking hard. At last he turned to me, and I noticed that his face had grown stern—and stubborn.

'No!' he said. 'I won't give you any word, or any promise. You must do what you please. But I'll say this—you'll make a mistake if you fix on him as either murderer or thief in this case. Of course he's innocent! Do what you please. And now, will you go away? I told you I could only give you a few minutes.'

I went away, sorely upset and puzzled, and walked slowly back to my office. My clerk met me at the door.

'There's that young man that came with the young woman waiting for you, sir,' he said. 'James Collier. He wants to see you again. He's in your room—I told him you wouldn't be long.'

I went into my room—Collier sat on the edge of a chair, twiddling his cap and staring about him. At sight of me he rose, grinning sheepishly.

'Well, Jim?' I said. 'What now?'

He dropped into his chair again, and making an effort spoke.

'Ellen,' he said. 'Ellen, she didn't tell all there was to tell. Left a bit out, like. So I thought——'

'What did she leave out?' I asked.

'Come to think of it, I did, after we'd been here,' he continued. 'But she'd gone, then. So I concluded to come myself. Thinking it might be important.'

'Quite right, Jim; much obliged to you,' I said. 'And what is it?'

It required a minute or two of severe mental effort on Jim's part to bring himself to the arduous task of accurate statement. As Ellen had remarked, he was not a great hand with his tongue. His memory, however, seemed to be in excellent condition.

'It was like this here,' he began. 'Ellen, she forgot to tell about something else we saw. About—him, you know.'

'Young Mr Richard?' I suggested.

'That's it! Him!' he assented. 'When he come into the wood, through the gate, and shoved his bike atween the hedge and them shrubs—I can show you the place—there was something that Ellen didn't tell about.'

'Yes?' I said, patiently. 'What was it, Jim?'

'He took a stick off his bicycle—strapped along the centre bar, it was,' he continued. 'A walking-stick! Thick 'un—I saw it plain.'

'How could you see it?' I asked. 'It was ten o'clock at night and dark.'

'Aye, but he'd a bit o' difficulty with the strap or cord it was fastened on with,' he answered. 'He took the lamp off the front of the bike to look at it. I saw the stick, plain enough. And the parcel.'

'What parcel?' I asked.

'He'd a parcel, tied on behind,' he replied. 'He took that off too.'

'Big parcel?' I inquired.

He held out his hands.

'About that square,' he said. 'Brown paper parcel.'

'Well?' I went on. 'What did he do then? With the stick and the parcel?'

'Carried 'em off with him into the wood, after he'd turned his lamp off,' he answered.

'What did there seem to be in the parcel?' I asked. 'Any idea?'

'No, I've no idea,' he said. 'Squarish sort o' parcel. In brown paper.'

'You're certain about this—especially about the stick?'

'I'm certain! It was a strong lamp, that. Saw everything.'

'Do you think you'd know that stick if you saw it again, Jim?' I asked.

But he shook his head at that.

'Ah, I dunno as I would!' he answered. 'Good thick 'un, it was.

But one stick's uncommon like another. 'Twasn't one o' your fancy walking-sticks. Plain stick.'

'Heavy enough to stun anybody, eh?'

'Oh, aye, it 'ud be strong enough for that,' he said. 'As I said, a thick 'un. Tied on to the bike it was. Likewise the parcel. Ellen, she forgot that bit.'

I sent him away, again bidding him to hold his tongue, and looked at my watch. It was not yet half-past two and there were several hours of daylight left. I already had a whole posse of men searching in and about Hagsdene Wood, but now I gathered together some more, all that I had available, and, going there with them myself, set to work on a thorough search of the undergrowth, the rabbit-warrens, the banks and hedgerows. For it seemed to me that the murderer would, in all probability, have thrown away his weapon (in the opinion of the doctors, a blunt one of some sort) as soon as he had made use of it.

At half-past five that afternoon one of my men, searching near Hebb's cottage, found a stick thrust into a rabbit's burrow. It was a plain, very heavy oak walking-stick, formidable enough—as my sergeant observed, you could have felled an ox with it. He and I returned to the town with it wrapped in his cape. Near the entrance to the wood we met Mr Radford's managing clerk, Hebb, returning to his home and his wife at the conclusion of his day's labours. A sudden impulse prompted me to show him the stick, and to ask him if he'd ever seen it before. I saw at once that he recognized it.

'Yes,' he said. 'It's a stick that I gave to Dick Radford last year, when he and I went on a bit of a walking tour. Certain of that. Dead certain!'

8

I had telephoned the news of Maidment's murder to our Chief Constable, Colonel Patterson, earlier in the day, and when I got back from my afternoon's lengthy visit to Hagsdene Wood he had just arrived in Ullathwaite and was at my office. At his suggestion I sent over for Mr Murwood, the solicitor, who was clerk to the local magistrates, and the three of us sat down and discussed the evidence I had collected during the day. The Chief Constable's face grew graver and graver as he listened to all I had to tell.

'It looks bad!' he muttered, as I came to the end of the story. 'It looks very bad! What do you make of it, Murwood?'

Murwood had been making notes of what I told them. He took up a sheet of paper.

'Summarized, it comes to just this,' he replied. 'I'll put it in sequence:

(i) Maidment is found dead in Hagsdene Wood early in the morning of October 18. Medical examination shows that he has been killed by blows on the head from some blunt weapon—any one of which blows was sufficient to cause instantaneous death.

(ii) Maidment, who was a rent-collector, is known to have collected about £112 in rents from tenants at Hagsdene Park during the evening of October 17. Some of this money was in gold, and one of the gold coins was a sovereign through which a very small hole had been bored.

(iii) Maidment is known to have left Hagsdene Park about a quarter past ten o'clock. He would be in Hagsdene Wood about twenty minutes later.

(iv) There is dependable evidence from two credible witnesses that Richard Radford entered Hagsdene Wood from the east side about ten o'clock on the evening in question. After hiding his bicycle and taking from it a parcel and a heavy stick he was seen to go across the wood in the direction of Mr Hebb's cottage, near which, next morning, Maidment's dead body was found.

(v) At ten-thirty on the morning of October 18 Richard Radford paid to Fardale, a well-known bookmaker of Ullathwaite, the sum of fifty-one pounds, of which six pounds was paid in sovereigns. Among these was the perforated sovereign which had been handed to Maidment the previous evening.

(vi) Mr John Radford, interviewed by Superintendent Henderson, declared that his son was not in or near Ullathwaite from six o'clock in the evening of October 17 until about ten o'clock on the morning of October 18. This, on inquiry, proved to be not true.

(vii) Richard Radford, asked for an explanation, admitted that he did not go to Lowsthorpe, where his father had said he had gone, but refused to say where he had been during the night. He also admitted that he had paid fifty-one pounds to Fardale, but refused to say how the gold, among which was the marked sovereign, came into his possession. He further admitted that he was in Hagsdene Wood at ten o'clock on the evening of October 17, but declined to say for what purpose. He declared emphatically that he neither murdered nor robbed Maidment, and refused to say more.

(vii) During the afternoon of October 18 a stick, a heavy oak walking-stick, which, in the opinion of the doctors, was probably the weapon used by Maidment's assailant, was discovered by a constable in Hagsdene Wood, where it had been concealed in a rabbit-burrow. This has been identified by Mr Ralph Hebb, managing clerk to Mr John Radford, as a stick which he presented to Mr Richard Radford last year.

That's all—so far,' concluded Murwood. 'And—enough!'

The three of us sat for a moment in silence.

'What's to be done?' asked the Chief Constable at last. 'Miserable affair! Isn't Mr Radford senior Mayor of Ullathwaite? And very much respected?'

'Both, sir,' I replied. 'And he's just about to be re-elected Mayor for another term of office.'

'And this lad?' he went on. 'What do you know of him, Henderson?'

'He has the reputation of being a bit wild,' I answered. 'A rather rackety youngster. But murder!—that's a very different thing.'

'Mayn't have ever meant murder,' remarked Murwood. 'He may have meant only to stun him, so that he could get the money. Do you know if Fardale had been putting the screw on him pretty tight?'

'Fardale,' I replied, 'had certainly given him an ultimatum. He'd told him that if he didn't pay up by eleven o'clock this morning he would tell Mr Radford senior all about it, and would refuse any further business with him, Richard. I don't suppose the second threat bothered Richard a scrap—there are half a dozen bookmakers in Ullathwaite he could bet with. But I think he'd be frightened about the other threat.'

'Ever been in any trouble before?' asked the Chief Constable. 'Ever been in your hands, for instance, for anything?'

'Mine, no!' I answered. 'Certainly not! Nor with the borough police, either, as far as I'm aware.'

'No, no!' said Murwood. 'There's nothing of that sort against him. Just a wild young shaver—that's about all.'

'Well, what's to be done?' repeated the Chief Constable. 'Is there, on this evidence, a *prima facie* case; one that would justify his arrest?'

'Decidedly there is,' replied Murwood. 'Circumstantial evidence, of course, but it's pretty strong.'

'What do you think, Henderson?' asked the Chief Constable. 'You've seen him already. What's your honest opinion?'

That was a stiff question. It was also one that I had been putting to myself over and over again, all the afternoon, ever since the moment in which Dick Radford had stormed angrily out of the Mayor's Parlour, slamming the door on me and his father.

'I don't know what to think, sir,' I replied. 'I'm undecided and uneasy. I suppose that what I do really think is this—I can't bring myself to believe the lad guilty of murder. But—I think he knows something; something that he will not and cannot be made to tell.'

'Shielding somebody?' suggested Murwood.

'Maybe!' I said. 'He's as stubborn and obstinate as ever they make 'em. I could see that his father would get nothing out of him. Perhaps his mother——'

The Chief Constable's face brightened.

'Good idea!' he exclaimed. 'Now look here! What do you say if the three of us call at Mr Radford's private residence and see if we can't bring some family influence to bear on this lad? Of course, if he won't speak——'

'I don't think he will, sir, unless his mother has more influence over him than his father has,' I said. 'But we can try. It's not far to the Mayor's house.'

'Let's go, then,' said the Chief Constable. 'Nasty business! But we may as well get on with it.'

We went off, there and then, to Mr Radford's. He lived in a big house, standing in its own grounds, on the outskirts of the town. The smart parlourmaid who opened the door to us looked doubtful.

'Mr Radford's at dinner, sir,' she replied to the Chief Constable's inquiry.

'No matter; we must see him at once,' said the Chief Constable. 'Tell him that Colonel Patterson is here and wishes to see him without delay.'

A moment or two later we were shown into Mr Radford's study; he came to us without any further waiting on our part. He was outwardly cool and collected—and he said nothing. Closing the door behind him, he turned and looked at Patterson.

'Mr Radford,' began the Chief Constable, 'you will know already why we have called on you. Superintendent Henderson has put you in possession of certain facts. Have you persuaded your son to speak?'

Mr Radford looked slowly from one to the other of us.

'No!' he answered.

'Have you tried?'

'Yes!'

'Have you pointed out to him the dangerous position in which he finds himself?'

'He is aware of it—fully!'

'The evidence—circumstantial though it is—is very serious, Mr Radford. Does he realize that?'

'Yes!'

'And still he won't say anything?'

'He will say nothing!'

'That's—final?'

'Final!'

The Chief Constable hesitated and sighed.

'But consider, Mr Radford! We have been going into the evidence, we three. It's strong; some people would call it damning. Does he realize——?'

'I have told you that he will say nothing! Nothing, that is, beyond what he said to Superintendent Henderson, in my presence, this afternoon.'

'If he would only give some explanation, Mr Radford——'

'He will give no explanation!'

The Chief Constable shook his head.

'Well! Where is he, Mr Radford?'

'In my dining-room. We are at dinner.'

'He has made no attempt to go away, then?'

'Go away? Why should he go away? Do you think he's afraid? He has already told Henderson that he did not kill Maidment nor rob him, dead or alive! He has no intention of going away.'

'Mr Radford, why won't he tell us where he was last night, and where he got the money he paid to Fardale? If he would do that——'

'I have already told you he will not do that!'

'You're sure?'

'Have I not said that was final?'

'But supposing his mother asked him to tell?'

'She has already asked him to tell.'

'And?'

'That has made no difference.'

'You don't encourage him in this attitude of silence, Mr Radford?'

'I neither encourage him nor discourage him. My son is of age.

What I feel about it is this—if my son says, as he has said, that he did not kill Maidment nor rob him, I believe him!'

'Absolutely?'

'Absolutely! He is my son.'

'But supposing it was an accidental affair? That he only meant to stun him? Your son was hard-pressed for money.'

'I have told you that my son says that he did not rob Maidment, dead or alive. Your supposition, therefore, is baseless.'

Colonel Patterson looked at me, and from me to Murwood. I am afraid he got no help from either of us, and he turned to the Mayor again.

'This is one of the most painful things I have ever had to do with!' he exclaimed. 'Well, may we see him, Mr Radford—and your wife?'

The Mayor hesitated a moment. Then he opened the door and, motioning us to follow him, led us across the hall into the dining-room. There was Mrs Radford, and there was her daughter, and there was her son. And to all appearance they were dining unconcernedly.

'Dick!' said Mr Radford. 'Colonel Patterson wants to speak to you.'

Dick looked round.

'Well?' he said.

'Mr Richard,' said the Chief Constable, 'I want to appeal to you in your mother's presence! Will you tell us the truth about this affair, or what you know of it? Will you clear yourself? Will you speak?'

Dick looked his questioner full in the face.

'No!' he answered.

Colonel Patterson turned to Mrs Radford.

'Mrs Radford,' he said, 'you are his mother! Ask him to reconsider——'

Mrs Radford looked quietly at all three of us.

'I have asked him,' she said. 'He will say nothing. But I am sure of this—he is innocent of either murder or robbery. And, as you say, I'm his mother.'

There was no more said. Patterson, Murwood, and I walked out of the room and the house. Once outside, Patterson wiped the sweat off his face.

'Well!' he said. 'There's only one thing to be done! Get on with it, Henderson!'

9

We arrested Richard Radford that night. That he and his family evidently expected it was plain from the fact that he was ready for us when we called again, and that his mother had packed a small suitcase containing immediate necessities. He said nothing when arrested, and nothing when formally charged, and I saw quite well that the policy of defiant silence which he had adopted from the first was going to be maintained until the end.

He was brought up before the West Riding magistrates, sitting at Ullathwaite, next morning. Intense interest had already been aroused in the town and in the neighbourhood, and the courthouse was packed. There was an unusually full bench; Mr Wrenne presided. But the proceedings on that occasion were merely formal and therefore very brief. Evidence of arrest was given and a remand asked for and granted: the whole thing was over in a few minutes. But later in the day the coroner's inquest on Maidment was opened, and the proceedings at that lasted until evening. All the evidence we had accumulated was brought forward before the coroner and his jury: everybody in the town, accordingly, became familiar with it. Possibly, had the coroner desired it, he could have got a verdict from his jury there and then, but he, remarking that he should not sit again until after the adjourned police proceedings, adjourned his own inquiry for three weeks.

Next morning the local newspaper came out with a verbatim report of the proceedings before the coroner, and every man and woman in Ullathwaite began to talk and to talk of nothing else. From what I heard, and from what was reported to me, it soon became evident that the vast majority of Ullathwaite people were on Dick Radford's side. What the general attitude was I soon discovered from a conversation I had with a certain well-known man of the town, a somewhat eccentric, but eminently shrewd, keen-witted business man who was a great figure on the Town Council. Meeting me in the market-place two or three days after Dick Radford had been remanded in custody, he buttonholed me.

'Now, Mr Superintendent,' he said, 'what are you making out about this murder case? Anything fresh?'

'Nothing more than you have no doubt read in the local paper,' I replied.

'What do you think, yourself?' he demanded.

'That is not for me to say,' I answered.

'Oh!' he said. 'Well, I know what I think!'

'Yes?' I rejoined. 'I should be glad to hear your opinion.'

'Would you?' he retorted. 'Maybe—and maybe not! For my opinion is that you're on the wrong tack!'

'Can you suggest the right one?' I asked.

'Yes, I can!' he said. 'Get off the wrong 'un to begin with! Young Dick no more killed that Maidment chap than I did! No, nor robbed his dead body either! Anybody that knows him knows well enough where the truth lies!'

'Where, then?' I asked. 'I would give something to know, myself.'

He seized the lapel of my coat again, and shook it vigorously.

'Lord bless you!' he said vehemently. 'Can't you see? Where are your eyes—and your brains? The lad's shielding somebody! Who? God bless my life and soul!—that's your job! Find out who it is! What're you there for?'

10

This was all very well, but not so easy of accomplishment as the worthy gentleman seemed to suggest. There was not the slightest clue to any possible murderer of Roger Maidment other than Dick Radford. By that time I had raked up every scrap of information available about Maidment. He was a quiet, inoffensive fellow, little known in the town, who appeared to have kept himself to himself and to have mixed very little with Ullathwaite people. I could not learn that he had had any enemies; the sum of my investigations amounted to this—Maidment undoubtedly had been attacked and (possibly accidentally) killed for the sake of the money he had on him. And if Dick Radford was not his assailant, then there was nothing whatever to show who was.

Between Dick's first appearance before the magistrates and the second, Colonel Patterson and I spent hours in discussing the facts of the case. This was certain: At ten o'clock on the evening of the murder Dick Radford, carrying a stick and a parcel, disappeared into Hagsdene Wood in the direction of Hebb's cottage, and from that time until he turned up at his father's office in Ullathwaite next morning—somewhere, as far as I could ascertain, about half-past nine, he being the first arrival there that morning—his whereabouts was absolutely unknown to anyone but himself. Where had he spent the night? What had he done with his parcel? What did it contain? It was certain that he had not gone to Mr Verrill's at Lowsthorpe; equally certain that he had not returned home. Where, then, had he been? Where was he going when Jim Collier and Ellen Hopkinson saw him enter the wood, into the thickest part of which he disappeared?

'Where is there, about there, that he could go?' asked Colonel Patterson as we discussed these questions. 'What houses are there near Hagsdene Wood?'

I had caused a carefully drawn map of the vicinity of Hagsdene Wood to be prepared by the county surveyor, and I now placed it before him.

'This will make things clear, sir,' I said, proceeding to point out the various points. 'This is a map of, say, a square mile, or perhaps rather more, round the scene of the murder. Here, on the east side of Hagsdene Wood, is the spot where Collier and his sweetheart saw Richard Radford leave his bicycle and enter the wood. He went in this direction, along this woodland path towards Hebb's cottage. He would pass the exact place, marked there, where Maidment's dead body was found. He——'

'A moment,' interrupted Colonel Patterson. 'How long would it take him to walk from where Collier and the girl saw him to the place where the body lay?'

'Three minutes—I have had it timed exactly,' I replied.

'And they say that they saw him at ten o'clock?' he asked.

'Ellen Hopkinson said it would be all about ten o'clock,' I answered. 'But Collier was more precise. He said it was exactly ten o'clock, for he heard the Town Hall clock strike.'

'Do you know what time Maidment left Hagsdene Park?'

'Yes—I have made the most searching inquiries. He certainly did not leave the last house he called at before a quarter past ten.'

'And it would take him how long to reach the place where his body was found?'

'From fifteen to twenty minutes' sharpish walking.'

'That means that he wouldn't reach this place in the wood till about half-past ten or twenty-five to eleven. In that case, supposing young Radford to be guilty, he must have lain in wait for Maidment for something like half an hour?'

'Exactly, sir: that is the theory.'

'Well, now, supposing he didn't wait at all; that he is, as he affirms, absolutely innocent—where could he go? He went through the wood, or the path by Hebb's cottage—what lies beyond? There, I suppose, are the houses marked here? Whose are they?'

I picked up my pencil again and began to particularize.

'Beyond Hebb's cottage, sir, which is at the western edge of the wood, there is a wide meadow that slopes down to a narrow valley. Along this, backed by the meadow, there are four—no, five—very good houses, all detached, all standing in their own grounds. This is Colonel Wharton's. This is Mr Walkingham's: he, as you know, is manager of the Ullathwaite and District Bank. This is Mr Norrington's. I don't know if you know him—he is an elderly gentleman who bought this property about a year ago; he has a very pretty wife, who is much younger than himself: she made rather a sensation in our amateur dramatic society's performances last winter.'

'I remember, I remember!' agreed Colonel Patterson. 'Oh, yes, I know Norrington. Used to be on the Stock Exchange—met him now and then since he came here. Well, and these other two houses?'

'That is Mr John Pratt's—he's a retired tradesman, who was Mayor a few years since. And this, the last one, is Mr Garland's—he's also a retired man.'

'Made any inquiry at these houses?'

'Oh, at all of them! We've made every inquiry we could think of, all round the district. No one can tell us anything of young Radford's whereabouts that night. None of the people in these houses saw or heard of him. And, as you see, beyond these five houses there is nothing but open country.'

'He must have been accommodated in the town,' muttered the Colonel. 'Somebody harboured him, and is keeping the secret. But there's another thing, Henderson,' he went on suddenly. 'What about his father's office? Probably he had a key to it? He could have gone there.'

'No, sir,' I replied. 'I thought of that. Mr Radford's office is in strict charge of a caretaker and his wife. They assure me that it would be an absolute impossibility for anyone to enter that office at night without their knowledge. Moreover, they mentioned to me that Mr Radford senior, on that particular night, came himself to the office very late and was working there till one o'clock in the morning. According to them, he has often done this since his election to the mayoralty, to make up for the time he has to spend at the Town Hall on Corporation business. So Dick, in any case, would not have turned in there.'

'Well, it's a mystery, Henderson!' said Colonel Patterson. 'He went somewhere, that's certain. And there's no doubt about it—somewhere, somebody knows a lot; somebody who won't come forward!'

'I'm beginning to think so,' I said. 'But who?'

That question still remained unanswered when Dick Radford was again brought before the magistrates. This time the whole of the evidence against him was brought forward; the proceedings lasted the better part of a day. His father had entrusted his defence, in the first place, to Mr Wilsborough, a rising young solicitor in the town, who was believed to have a big future before him; Mr Wilsborough, having found out beyond question that his client was absolutely adamant in his resolve not to speak, wisely confined himself to pleading not guilty and reserving his defence. And at five o'clock that afternoon Richard Radford was formally committed to take his trial for the murder of Roger Maidment at the ensuing Grandminster Assizes.

Mr Wrenne was again the presiding magistrate, and when the case was over he sent for Colonel Patterson, Mr Wilsborough, myself, and the prosecuting solicitor, asking us to join him in his room. He was alone there, and as soon as we had entered he unlocked a drawer in his desk and produced a letter.

'I want to show you gentlemen a communication which I received this morning,' he said. 'I found it here when I came to court. Now, first look at the envelope, carefully. You will notice, to begin with, that the address "To the Chairman of the Magistrates, West Riding Court House, Ullathwaite, Yorkshire," is typewritten. You will notice, further, that the letter was posted, yesterday, in the S.W. district of London. Now,' he went on, drawing a square sheet of notepaper from the envelope and spreading it out on his desk, 'notice, next, that the letter enclosed in the envelope is also typewritten and has no signature, not even a pseudonym, attached. Read it!'

The four of us crowded together and read what lay before us.

> The writer, who is obliged to remain anonymous, desires the kind attention of the Ullathwaite magistrates to the following:
>
> 1. Richard Radford is absolutely innocent of the crime with which he is charged.
>
> 2. According to the newspapers Roger Maidment was murdered in Hagsdene Wood about half-past ten on the night of October 17. From a quarter past ten onwards Richard Radford was not near the scene of the murder, though he probably passed it a few minutes after ten o'clock on his way elsewhere.
>
> 3. If the worst comes to the worst Richard Radford's

innocence of either murder or robbery can, *and will be*, proved to the full.

'What do you make of that?' asked Mr Wrenne. 'As it is an anonymous letter I have not shown it to anyone.'

Nobody answered this question. The prosecuting solicitor and Mr Wilsborough looked at each other. What they were thinking nobody knows. The prosecuting solicitor, however, spoke suddenly, addressing Wilsborough.

'Is your client going to keep up his policy of saying nothing?' he asked.

'As far as I am aware—yes!' replied Wilsborough.

'I don't want that!' said the prosecuting solicitor, pointing to the letter.

'I do!' said Wilsborough.

Mr Wrenne handed it over. We all went away, wondering.

11

I don't know what Mr Wilsborough did with the letter handed to him by Mr Wrenne. As far as I can recollect, I never heard of it again. Possibly he showed it to Mr Radford senior; he may have shown it to Dick Radford. It was certainly not mentioned at the trial. Before that, however, Colonel Patterson and myself had discussed it.

'Do you know what I think, Henderson?' said the Colonel. 'I think that letter was written, or, rather, caused to be typed by somebody who lives in Ullathwaite or in the neighbourhood of Ullathwaite.'

'It was posted in London,' I remarked.

'That's easy enough!' he said. 'The author of it had gone up to town. Now if we could find out if anybody—I mean anybody of importance—in the town or neighbourhood has been up in London lately——'

'There are no end of people who are constantly running up to London,' I interrupted. 'And you're forgetting another thing, sir—what could be easier than to send that typewritten document to some friend in London with instructions to post it there, and even in a particular district? Nothing! But why anybody of importance?'

'It was the letter of an educated person,' he answered. 'The arrangement and phraseology, I mean. A man's work, in my opinion!'

'Why not a woman's?' I asked.

'No!' he said. 'It was too clearly, too systematically arranged. A man sent it. Now where the devil did young Radford spend the night of the 17th? Somewhere close at hand, of course. But where? With whom? And why this mystery about it? Perhaps they'll let it out, and clear everything up when it comes to the trial.'

But when the trial came on at the Winter Assizes at Grandminster, before Mr Justice Selgrave, a notoriously severe judge, it very soon became evident that whatever pressure had been brought to bear upon him by relations, friends, and legal advisers, Dick Radford was going to stick like grim death to his policy of silence. His father had spared no expense in securing the services of one of the most eminent criminal lawyers of the day, Mr Henshawe, Q.C., and from what I picked up here and there I knew that Henshawe and Wilsborough, as solicitor instructing counsel, had spent hours and hours in preparing a defence—towards which Dick would give no help. Once I had occasion to see Dick myself while he was awaiting trial, and I spoke to him.

'Mr Richard,' I said, 'if you're innocent, as you say you are, why don't you tell the truth as to that night and be done with it? Think of the pain and anxiety you'd spare your people.'

He looked at me for a second as if he understood and was sorry; then his face set as hard as flint.

'No!' he said. 'Let the thing go on! No jury will ever find me guilty!'

'Suppose they do?' I suggested.

'Can't suppose it! They won't!' he retorted. 'You'll see!'

I wasn't as sure as he was. The tale, told by witness after witness, when the prosecution was opened, seemed a pretty damning one. Nothing could shake the evidence of Collingwood, nor of Fardale, nor of Jim Collier and Ellen Hopkinson. The first witness, indeed, that Mr Henshawe attacked was Hebb, who was called to prove that the stick found thrust away in a rabbit-burrow in Hagsdene Wood was the identical stick he had given to Richard Radford some time previously when they were starting out on a walking tour. Hebb was the sort of witness who swears promptly and positively—oh, yes, there wasn't the slightest doubt that that was the very stick. Then Henshawe took him in hand.

'How do you recognize this stick as the one you presented to the prisoner?' he asked.

'I recognize it,' replied Hebb. 'It is the stick!'

'Yes—but, how? Did you put any mark on it?'

'No!'

'It is a very common sort of stick. Just a plain oak stick, with a rather pronounced knob at the end where one handles it. What difference is there between this stick and scores of similar sticks?'

'That's the stick I gave him!'

'How much did you give for it?'

'A shilling!'

'Where did you buy it?'

'At Shillaker's, in Waingate.'

'Was it one of a similar lot of oak sticks? In a bundle, eh?'

'I—I think so.'

'Supposing we put it back in such a bundle and mixed them up—do you think you could pick it out?'

'I know that's the stick I bought and gave Mr Richard!'

'Yes, but I want to know *how* you know! Tell us!'

'It *is* the stick!'

Mr Henshawe sat down. The case for the prosecution came to an end: Mr Henshawe began his opening speech for the defence. It was a very brief one—but it contained one important announcement. His client absolutely refused to give evidence. Not one word would anyone get out of him. And when they heard that, there were people in court who believed that the thing was as good as over, and that presently they would hear Dick Radford sentenced to death.

Mr Henshawe, however, went quietly on his way, and presently called his first witness, Ephraim Shillaker, a tobacconist and stick and umbrella merchant. Things began to be interesting.

'You see this stick, Mr Shillaker? The witness Hebb swears that he bought it from you, last year. Did he?'

'Very likely! I can't say, positively. I sell scores of sticks like this in the course of a year. Common as blackberries! A shilling each.'

'Just an ordinary, cheap, handy stick, eh? A popular line. Are these oak sticks pretty much alike?'

'Like as two peas!'

'If the stick you're now examining were put in a bundle with a dozen similar sticks, could you pick it out?'

'No, and nobody else! Impossible!'

'All these cheap oak sticks, at a shilling, so closely resemble each other?'

'That's it!'

'If you picked one up, in a wood, or a field, or by the roadside, you wouldn't like to swear that it was a stick with which you were familiar?'

'No, of course not!'

'Have you any of these oak sticks in your shop at present?'

'Several bundles of 'em. I've brought one, picked up at random, with me.'

An usher came forward with a bundle of sticks: Mr Henshawe spent five minutes in exhibiting it to his lordship and the jury. Then he put a final question to Mr Shillaker.

'Mr Shillaker, do you think it possible that anybody could positively identify this particular stick as being a stick he'd bought a year previously?'

'No, sir! Impossible! Unless, indeed, he'd put a mark on it. There's no mark anywhere on this stick. And,' concluded Mr Shillaker as he turned to leave the witness-box, 'I may say that there's scores and scores of these shilling oak sticks in Ullathwaite at this minute! I've sold over two hundred in the past three years—and they're stocked at other shops than mine.'

'Thank you, Mr Shillaker,' said Mr Henshawe. 'Call William Brewer.'

A quiet-mannered, rather shy-looking man entered the box and after taking the oath turned in counsel's direction.

'Mr Brewer,' said Henshawe, 'you are manager of Messrs W. H. Smith & Son's bookstall at Ullathwaite Railway Station?'

'I am.'

'Do you remember the afternoon of October 17?'

'Quite clearly!'

'How do you fix your remembrance of it, Mr Brewer?'

'By the fact that it was the day preceding the murder in Hagsdene Wood.'

'Did young Mr Radford, Mr Richard Radford, come to your bookstall that afternoon?'

'Yes! He came there about half-past four.'

'For what purpose? What did he want?'

'He came to see if I'd got him three new novels which he'd ordered about a week previously.'

'Had you?'

'Yes. They'd come in that morning.'

'What novels were they? The titles, I mean—and authors.'

Here came in a dramatic interruption. Dick Radford, who, I could see, had viewed the appearance of Mr Brewer with something very like dismay, sprang to the front of the dock with a sharp exclamation.

'Stop that! Don't tell, Brewer! Do you hear, don't tell! Keep your mouth shut!'

Before the judge could speak Henshawe seized on the situation.

'I withdraw that question,' he said quickly. 'Well—did he take them away with him?'

'Yes. I made them up into a parcel for him, and he took them away.'

'Pay for them?'

Mr Brewer smiled quietly.

'Not yet,' he answered.

'Was he in the habit of buying new novels from you?'

'Occasionally. Notable novels.'

'These, then—were they notable?'

'They were novels recently published, about which people were talking a good deal.'

'You don't know what he was going to do with them?'

'No, sir I do not.'

Mr Henshawe signified that he had done with Mr Brewer. He looked round the court. His next words came as a surprise.

'Call Miss Audrey Radford!'

Audrey Radford came forward. I knew her as a very pretty, somewhat shy girl: on this occasion, however, she looked calm, composed, assured.

'Miss Radford,' said Henshawe, after the usual preliminaries, 'you remember the afternoon and evening of October 17 last?'

'Very well indeed!'

'Did you see your brother Richard that evening at about a quarter to six?'

'I did!'

'Where?'

'In the hall of our house.'

'What was he doing?'

'He was tying a parcel on his bicycle.'

'Did you ask him what was in the parcel?'

'Yes!'

'What did he reply?'

'He asked me what business of mine it was. Then he said it was some books he was going to take to somebody.'

'Did you ask what books?'

'Yes.'

'Well—did he tell you?'

'No! He said I might be blowed, or something of that sort.'

'Then you don't know what books he had in that parcel?'

'No, but I know he'd got them from Smith's, because I saw their label on the parcel.'

'Well, you say he was fastening the parcel on his bicycle. Did he tell you where he was going?'

'No. But I'd heard him say something at lunch about going to see Mr Verrill at Lowsthorpe, and spending the night there.'

'Well, Miss Radford, did you see your brother fasten anything else on his bicycle before leaving the house?'

'Yes.'

'What?'

'A walking-stick. He fastened it to the cross-bar. I've often seen him do that when he was going into the country.'

'Look carefully at this stick, Miss Radford. Is that the stick you saw your brother fasten on his bicycle?'

'No, most certainly not! This is an oak stick, stained or painted yellow. The stick he fastened on his machine was a thick ash-plant, green, of course.'

'You swear that?'

'Certainly!'

'Look at this oak stick again. Do you recognize it?'

'No—we have several sticks, just like it, knocking about the place. Half a dozen, I should think. I have bought two or three myself, at Shillaker's, at one time or another.'

'But—once more—the stick which your brother fastened on his machine was—on your oath!—a thick ash-plant, in its natural bark?'

'Yes!'

Mr Henshawe bowed Miss Radford out of the box.

'Call James Collier again!'

Jim Collier re-entered the witness-box. Henshawe showed him the oak stick.

'Collier—on your oath!—can you swear that this is the stick you saw Richard Radford take off his bicycle that night in Hagsdene Wood?'

'No, sir!'

'You swear that he took off a stick, but you cannot swear that it was this stick?'

'That's it, sir! All I know is he took off a stick, a thick stick. But I couldn't swear to the stick itself, sir.'

Henshawe called no further witnesses. He made a very short closing speech: his line was that Dick Radford knew nothing about the murder and that he had what he considered honourable reasons of his own for concealing his whereabouts on the night of October 17. Then followed the closing speech for the prosecution: it merely reviewed the circumstantial evidence. And then Mr Justice Selgrave summed up. My impression was that his summing-up went dead against the prisoner.

12

The jury retired at three o'clock in the afternoon. They were still in retirement at six o'clock; still locked in their room at nine. But at a quarter to ten they came back. There was a painful silence as the clerk of assize put the fateful question: a worse and far more painful as his last word was spoken.

Then we heard the foreman of the jury answer:

'*Not Guilty!*'

II

THE DEFENCE IS SILENCE

(Statement of Mr E. H. Wilsborough, Solicitor, of Ullathwaite)

As the Solicitor entrusted with the preparation of the defence, and at the request of Mr P. W. Wrenne, Chairman of our local bench of magistrates of the West Riding, sitting at Ullathwaite, I proceed to set down all that I know of the arrest, examination before the magistrates, and trial at the Grandminster Assizes of Richard Radford, charged with the murder of Roger Maidment at Hagsdene Wood on the night of October 17, 1899.

On October 14 I went up to London on legal business and was detained there until late in the afternoon of October 18. I left town by the 5.30 train, and arrived at Ullathwaite four hours later. I was sitting in my dining-room at ten o'clock over a late supper when my parlourmaid came to tell me that Mr John Radford, the Mayor of Ullathwaite, and a prominent member of my own profession, was in the hall and wished to see me immediately: I bade her bring him in to me at once.

I saw—as soon as he entered the room—that Mr Radford was in a state of high nervous tension. But it was manifested—to me—by the unusual and quite unnatural calmness of his manner. His face was set and stern, and his voice, when he spoke, cold and formal.

'You have been away, Wilsborough?' he said as he took the chair I offered him. 'For some days?'

'Four days—in town,' I replied. 'Only got in half an hour ago.'

'You have not yet heard of anything that has happened—here—since you went away?'

'Not yet. Has anything happened?'

He turned his hat over on his knee: I fancied I detected a slight trembling of his hands.

'You would know Maidment, the rent-collector?' he asked.

'Maidment? Yes. What about him?' I replied. 'Run away?'

Again he turned his hat over, once or twice, eyeing me closely out of his eye-corners.

'Maidment,' he answered, 'was found dead this morning in Hagsdene Wood. He had been murdered—and robbed.'

I stared at him in amazement.

'Good heavens!' I exclaimed. 'And——'

He cleared his throat with a slight cough.

'The police,' he said, with an effort—'the police have arrested my son—Richard!'

I was lifting some food to my lips when he said this, but I paused in the action and, dropping the fork back on the plate, rose to my feet—why, I can't say. I went over to where he sat on the hearth.

'You don't mean it!' I said. 'Dick!'

I knew Dick Radford well enough—after all, I was only a few years his senior. He was a bit wild and rakish, but nothing would ever have induced me to suspect him of murder—nor of theft.

'He was arrested an hour ago,' he answered, simply. 'He is at the cells in the West Riding police court.'

'Some mistake, of course,' I said. 'What does Dick say? Denies it, I'm sure! And Dick's truthful.'

'On the whole, yes,' replied Dick's father. 'He has told me lies, to be sure, now and then. But I should call him truthful—if it comes to it. He has stated, unequivocally, that he did not kill Maidment or rob him, alive or dead. I believe him.'

'But the ground for arrest?' I said. 'What evidence is there against him? Is there—any?'

He shook his head at that, and I began to see that behind his effort at calmness there was a good deal of mental agitation.

'Circumstantial evidence!' he answered. 'There is circumstantial evidence. I had better tell you all I know. Henderson—the police superintendent—has told me of all that is known to him. It is just this: Yesterday evening, Maidment, following his usual practice, went to collect the monthly rent of that new property at Hagsdene Park. He collected about a hundred pounds—perhaps rather more. Some of the tenants paid him by cheque; some in notes; some in gold. One tenant, Collingwood——'

'I know Collingwood,' I interrupted. 'A dependable man!'

'Collingwood paid him in gold, giving him six sovereigns,' Mr Radford went on. 'One of these sovereigns had a small hole drilled in it. Collingwood noticed it when he was paying it over and drew Maidment's attention to it—Maidment pooh-poohed it and accepted it. Maidment went away from Hagsdene Park, with this hundred pounds or so in his possession, about a quarter past ten last night. This morning, at an early hour, he was found dead in Hagsdene Wood—and there was no money.'

'But—murder?' I said. 'How do they know it was murder?'

'He had received blows—heavy blows—on the head,' replied Mr Radford. 'Some blunt weapon. Any one of the blows would cause death, so the medical men say.'

'Why is Dick suspected?' I inquired.

He shook his head, slowly.

'It is very puzzling, very puzzling!' he answered. 'I had better tell you all I know from another angle. We understood at home yesterday evening that Dick was going to ride over on his bicycle to Lowsthorpe to spend the night at Verrill's. He said—Dick said—he was. But—that wasn't true. At any rate, he didn't go to Verrill's. He left home about six o'clock—where he went after that, I don't know. But at ten o'clock he was seen to enter Hagsdene Wood, and to go across towards the west side of it—he'd pass close by the place where Maidment's body was found. Where he went, then, no one knows; he will not say. But he spent the night somewhere—certainly not at home. And before ten o'clock this morning he was at my office. At half-past ten he went to see Fardale——'

'The bookmaker?'

'Exactly—turf commission agent he calls himself. It appears that, unknown to me, Dick has been betting. He owed Fardale fifty pounds—had owed him it for some little time. Fardale had been threatening him with exposure. Well, this morning he paid Fardale the fifty pounds. Part of the money he paid in gold. Among the gold was the perforated sovereign which Collingwood paid to Maidment the night before.'

'Good heavens!' I exclaimed. 'And I suppose Fardale—— But how did Fardale know anything about that?'

'Collingwood happened to meet Fardale at the Black Bull this morning, and told him, in discussing the murder, about the perforated coin. Fardale had the money which Dick had given him untouched in a certain pocket; he examined it and found that particular sovereign. Then he and Collingwood went to Henderson.'

'That's serious, Mr Radford!' I said. 'But—can't Dick explain? Won't he say where he got the sovereign?'

'He will give no answer whatever to these questions,' replied Mr Radford. 'He will not say where he spent last night. He will not say where he was between six o'clock yesterday evening and ten o'clock, when he was seen to enter Hagsdene Wood. And he will not say where he got the money to pay Fardale.'

'Not even where he got the marked sovereign?'

'No! He says that he knows nothing whatever about a marked sovereign. He admits that he gave Fardale some gold in paying the fifty pounds, but he swears that he never noticed any marked coin among it.'

'But why won't he tell?'

'I cannot tell you. But he won't!'

'But—you, his father? And—his mother? Won't he tell either, or both?'

'No! I am sure he will not—whatever happens!'

'A good deal may happen, Mr Radford. But what do you want me to do?'

'I want you to act for him—to prepare his defence. Of course they'll commit him to the Assizes.'

'You really think so?'

'I don't see how they can do anything else—on the evidence.'

'It's very suspicious, certainly. But if Dick's innocent, how did he get hold of that marked sovereign? Surely he could tell us that! In confidence, if in nothing else.'

'He will not tell, in confidence or in any other way or for any reason! I'm convinced of that. All he will say is that he knows nothing of Maidment's murder, did not murder him, did not rob him, never set eyes on him last night, alive or dead!'

'And you believe him?'

'Absolutely!'

'Then, Mr Radford, I think Dick is shielding some other person! What do you say?'

'I think it likely.'

'Do you think he knows who killed Maidment?'

Mr Radford reflected on this question during a brief silence.

'I think he may have a suspicion,' he replied at last.

'Have you asked him if he has?'

'No! He doesn't want to talk about it. His policy is silence.'

I thought matters over for a while.

'Do you wish me to see him to-night, Mr Radford?' I asked.

'No,' he answered, 'it is too late. But if you will see him in the morning, before the court proceedings begin——'

'Yes,' I said. 'I'll see him immediately after breakfast.'

He rose at that, and giving me a nod, shook hands, and went away in silence.

2

When Mr Radford had gone I sat down again to my interrupted supper, and while I ate I thought over what he had told me. And the more I thought the more I was convinced that I was confronted with what the story-tellers call a first-class mystery. I knew Dick Radford intimately—as I have said already, I was not many years his senior. He and I were fellow-cricketers, and I consequently saw a good deal of him. He was inclined to be a bit wild; I fancy he had been repressed, kept down, in his home-life; his father was a very precise, prim, stern sort of person; his mother was very Puritanical and religious. But between being mildly rakish—he had little chance to be more!—and being a murderer and a thief there is a vast difference: I could not bring myself to believe that Dick Radford would either rob or murder. Certainly the evidence against him which his father had outlined was grave—the perforated sovereign was a nasty thing to get over, though I saw at once that Fardale's testimony on that point would have to be scrutinized mercilessly. But if Dick knew himself to be wholly innocent, why this reticence about his movements and doings? What was it that made him keep silent—even from his own father and mother? A word or two from him as to where he had spent the night of October 17, where he had been at half-past ten that evening, where he had got the money to pay Fardale with, and we could establish a satisfactory alibi. Why wouldn't he speak? There could be but one answer to that question. Dick Radford, for reasons only known to himself, was keeping something back. What?

Nobody could say what but Dick. I went off to see him at his place of detention, the cells of the West Riding Court House, next morning. Before seeing him I saw Superintendent Henderson and told him Mr Radford had asked me to act on Dick's behalf. Henderson, a very humane and kindly man, shook his head.

'You'll be clever, Mr Wilsborough, if you can get anything out of him!' he remarked. 'I tried my best yesterday. A word or two from him, and he'd never have been where he is. Colonel Patterson tried his best, too, and it was no good. Why, he wouldn't even take any notice of his own mother's appeal! And if he wouldn't listen to her——'

'What's your opinion, Henderson?' I asked.

'Um!—that's a difficult one,' he replied. 'There's some nasty circumstantial evidence. For instance——'

'Mr Radford outlined it to me last night,' I interrupted. 'Some of it is—inconvenient.'

'That marked sovereign is awkward,' he went on. 'There's no doubt whatever that Collingwood paid it to Maidment, and no doubt at all that young Radford paid it to Fardale. How did young Radford get hold of it?'

'Have you got it?' I asked. 'Yes? Let me see it.'

He unlocked a drawer in his desk, took out a small cardboard box, and from it withdrew six sovereigns which he arranged in a row on his blotting-pad.

'There you are,' he said. 'Those are the coins which Dick Radford handed to Fardale. Fardale put them in a certain pocket, just as he'd received them, and never touched them until Collingwood told him about the perforated one. You see which that is?'

I saw the marked coin at once, of course. It had a very small hole drilled through it, just above the Queen's head and beneath the rim.

'And you say Collingwood will swear to his having handed that to Maidment?' I asked. 'Positively?'

'Positively!'

'And Fardale will swear that it was handed to him by Dick Radford?'

'Just as positively. They're both absolutely positive.'

'Well, take care of it, Henderson,' I said. 'And look here, Mr Radford told me last night that the rest of the money Dick paid to Fardale was in notes. Where are they?'

He pulled out a sealed envelope and proceeded to break the seal.

'They're here,' he answered. 'Fardale handed over to me the full amount of the money he'd received from Dick Radford: he'd never touched it since putting it in his pocket at the time of receipt until Collingwood told him of the marked sovereign. Now we've spoken of the money owing by Dick to Fardale as being fifty pounds, but as a matter of fact the precise amount was fifty-one pounds—a betting debt, you know. Dick handed him six pounds in gold and forty-five in Bank of England notes. Here are the notes, just as Fardale gave them into my keeping.'

I took the banknotes from him and turned them over. One thing struck me at once. There were nine notes of £5 each. Not a single note among the nine was a new one. All the notes showed signs of having been in circulation some little time; they were creased, thumbed, more or less soiled by usage.

'Look here, Henderson,' I said, handing them back, 'though you represent the other side and I'm to represent your prisoner, you won't mind telling me something? You say some of the residents at Hagsdene Park paid Maidment their rents in banknotes. Do you know if those who did took the numbers of the notes they gave him?'

'Well, I do!' he answered. 'They did not!—in any one case. Careless of them, of course, but—they didn't.'

'Have you shown them—that is, those who paid in notes—these particular notes?'

He hesitated a moment, as if chary of answering.

'It'll come out, you know, Henderson, if you have,' I said. 'You may as well tell me.'

'Well, I have,' he replied. 'Yes, I've shown them all round there.'

'Did anybody recognize any of these notes as notes paid by themselves to Maidment?' I asked. 'Come, now!'

'No!' he said. 'None of them. According to what they told me, they all seem to have given Maidment new notes, recently obtained from the banks.'

'Then these notes can't have been the notes which Maidment was carrying,' I said. 'All these nine notes have been used a good deal.'

'Yes,' he remarked. 'But—how do we know what money Maidment had on him? We do know that he collected about a hundred pounds at Hagsdene Park, but he may have had other money in his possession when he was struck down. Anyway, he certainly had that perforated sovereign. And there's not the slightest doubt, Mr Wilsborough, that that sovereign was handed by Dick Radford to Fardale the morning after the murder. Where did he get it?'

'I'm going to ask him that!' I replied.

'He won't tell you! He won't tell anything. His attitude puzzles me altogether. Why, he won't tell his own mother!'

'Well, you tell me something, Henderson,' I said. 'What do you police people know about Dick's movements on the evening and night of the 17th and the morning of the 18th?'

'No objection to telling you that,' he answered. 'In fact, I've no objection to telling you anything; it'll all come out. What we know is this—he left home at six o'clock on the evening of October 17, saying he was going to Mr Verrill's, at Lowsthorpe, some thirty miles away, for the night. He didn't go. He was seen—by two credible witnesses—to enter Hagsdene Wood at ten o'clock that night. We know nothing of any further movement or whereabouts of his until next morning when he called on Fardale about ten-thirty and paid his debt.'

'Thank you,' I said. 'Now I know where I am. And I'd better see my client at once before you take him into court. I suppose this morning's proceedings will be purely formal—evidence of arrest and so on and application for a remand in custody?'

'Just that, Mr Wilsborough,' he answered. 'Remand for a week.'

I got up to leave the room. But with my hand on the door I turned and looked at him.

'Henderson!' I said. 'Between ourselves, what do you think of this case?'

He stared at me for a second or two; then he shook his head.

'I'm absolutely licked by it!' he answered. 'I don't know what to think!'

3

The chiming of a clock in the market-place outside warned me that Henderson and I had been talking longer than I had intended and that there was now little time left before my client was due to appear in court.

'Well,' I said. 'I suppose I can see Dick?'

'Of course!' he answered. 'Whenever you like.'

'I should like to see him alone,' I suggested. 'I may be able to persuade him to talk.'

'I doubt it!' he said. 'My belief is that you might as well talk to a stone. You shall see him alone, though: I'll have him brought here to you.'

He left the room, and in a few minutes one of his sergeants opened the door and showed Dick Radford in. Dick gave me a sheepish grin. He reminded me of a boy who has been caught robbing an orchard and is half defiant and half deprecatory.

'Hullo, Wilsborough!' he said. 'What are you doing here?'

I had made up my mind as to my course of procedure, and I went straight to the point.

'You young ass!' I exclaimed. 'What are *you* doing here? That's the question—not what I'm doing here!'

'I didn't come here voluntarily,' he retorted. 'Had to!'

'Yes, and why?' I went on. 'Because you've got some damned quixotic notion in your silly head! Look here, my lad, you're no liar—in serious things, at any rate. You answer me two questions, on your honour. And remember that I shall believe what you say. One—did you kill Roger Maidment?'

He gave me a look that was almost a sneer, and his lip curled.

'No!' he answered.

'Did you rob him—alive or dead?'

'No!'

'Then what the devil are you doing here?' I said, angrily. 'Giving all this trouble to your father, mother, and sister, and causing no end of inconvenience and expense? Answer that!'

'How can I help it?' he replied. 'They suspect me and they collared me. They won't take my word, of course.'

'They'd take your word if you'd be reasonable and say where you were on the night of October 17 at the time Maidment was killed,' I said. 'You must have been somewhere near, and there's probably somebody who can prove it. There is, isn't there?'

He gave me a long, steady look.

'What have you come here for, Wilsborough?' he asked.

'Your father's employed me to act for you,' I answered. 'And I'm going to, and going to do all I can to save you from the possible consequences of your own stupidity. Come now, Dick, be reasonable! Tell me where you were at half-past ten that night, and with—whom.'

'No!' he answered.

'You won't?'

'I won't! Neither now nor at any time!'

'Look here, my lad,' I said, 'do you know that there's some very nasty evidence, of the sort styled circumstantial, against you? Very ugly evidence, in fact!'

'Quite aware of it,' he answered.

'Jurymen,' I continued, 'are uncertain creatures to deal with. And they're fond of solid facts. In this case there are some very unpleasant facts. On the face of it, there's a strong case against you, Dick. Now be sensible and tell me a few things. In confidence, you know—leaving me to judge how what you say should be made use of. You don't want your father, mother, sister——'

'What do you want to know?' he growled.

'First, did you leave your father's house at six o'clock on the evening of October 17?'

'Yes!'

'Saying you were going to Verrill's, at Lowsthorpe?'

'Yes.'

'You weren't, were you? Anyway, you didn't go?'

'I didn't go to Lowsthorpe.'

'Did you enter Hagsdene Wood at ten o'clock that night, Dick?'

'I did. Ten o'clock is quite right.'

'Well, where were you between six o'clock and ten o'clock?'

But he shook his head, smiling a little.

'No, Wilsborough, you won't get me! I shan't answer that!'

'Will you answer this? Where were you between ten o'clock and next morning?'

'I shan't tell you that, either!'

'Never?'

'Never! Under any consideration!'

'Will you tell me where you got the money with which to pay Fardale?'

'No!'

'But you admit that you did pay him?'

'Certainly I paid him. Fifty-one pounds. Forty-five in five-pound notes; six in gold.'

'Did you notice, amongst the gold, a sovereign through which a small hole had been drilled?'

'No! There may have been such a sovereign, but I never noticed it.'

'Well, come,' I continued, 'I think you might tell me where you got the gold, at any rate! Why not?'

'I shall not tell you!'

'The fact is, you won't tell me anything?' I said.

'I won't answer the questions you've just put!' he retorted.

'Will you answer this, then? Aren't you shielding somebody?'

'And I shan't answer that, either!' he said stubbornly. 'It's not a scrap of good, Wilsborough. I'm a pretty obstinate devil when it comes to it.'

'You're a damned young fool!' I exclaimed. 'Do you know that you're risking your neck, Master Dick Radford? I do, if you don't!'

'Um—I don't believe it,' he answered. 'I don't believe any jury will find me guilty. But anyway, you may as well know that I'm not going to answer any of the questions you've put—whoever puts them.'

'All right!' I said. 'We've got to save you from yourself. If we can!—that's just about it, my lad. If we can!'

4

The proceedings at Dick Radford's first appearance before the magistrates were purely formal; within an hour of their termination he was on his way to the detention prison at Grandminster. When he was next brought up before the Ullathwaite bench the prosecution unmasked its whole battery: we were treated to every scrap of circumstantial evidence that could be brought against us. Knowing that my client would certainly be committed for trial, I judged it wisest to reserve all defence until the Assizes. The fact of the case was that up to that moment I had very little, if anything, to offer on Dick Radford's behalf. I had not been able to elucidate the mystery of Maidment's murder; nothing had transpired to suggest that somebody other than Dick had attacked, killed, and robbed him; and I was certainly not in a position to set up an alibi. There was nothing for it but to let the case go for trial, and to endeavour in the meantime to save my obstinate client by clearing things up.

But just then something occurred which made me feel more convinced than ever that Dick Radford, from feelings of chivalry or honour or perhaps in order to keep an inconvenient secret, was shielding some other person. Mr Wrenne, chairman of the local bench of magistrates, received an anonymous typewritten letter, posted in London, the gist of which was that Dick Radford was absolutely innocent of the crime with which he was charged; that his innocence could be proved, and that 'if the worst came to the worst' his innocence *would* be proved. Mr Wrenne, after showing this letter to his fellow justices, to the Chief Constable, Colonel Patterson, to Superintendent Henderson, and to myself, handed it over to me at my request: nobody else seemed to feel any particular interest in it.

But I was deeply interested in it. I read it over and over again, and began to feel that it was a genuine letter, and that the writer firmly believed in what he or she had said. He or she—which? Was the writer a man or a woman? Something about the letter, something in the phraseology and in the almost threatening assurance of the whole thing made me incline to the opinion that it was of feminine origin. The mere fact that it had been posted in London did not impress me at all—it was an easy thing to send such a letter to London to be posted. But the idea that the sender was a woman, and one—according to her own assertion—in a position to prove Dick Radford's innocence was an important one. And that idea presently became strengthened in me by an interview with Dick's sister, Audrey.

Audrey Radford, whom I knew even better than I knew Dick, walked into my office one morning soon after Dick had been committed for trial at Grandminster Assizes, and told my clerk that she wanted a private talk with me.

As soon as we were alone she went straight to business.

'Look here!' she said. 'What's being done for Dick?'

I suppose I gave her an inquiring look. She went on talking before I could answer her question.

'Of course I know what you'll say, Ernest,' she continued. (She and I, being not much removed from each other in point of age and having known each other from the short-frock and knickerbocker stage, always used our Christian names.) 'You'll say that everything's being done that can be done! But what?'

'We could do a great deal more, Audrey, if Dick would do something for himself,' I answered. 'But up to now Dick will do nothing for himself.'

'If you mean that Dick should tell,' she replied, 'Dick won't!'

'You think he's got something to tell?' I suggested.

'Heaps!—of course,' she answered. 'But you'll not get him to say a word. I know Dick!'

'Obstinate as they make 'em,' I remarked. 'Stupid as a mule. Well, what's your opinion, Audrey?'

She gave me a knowing look.

'My opinion is that there's a woman in the case,' she replied.

'Yes?' I said. 'What woman?'

'As if I knew that! If I did know——'

'You'd split?'

'To save Dick, yes!'

I waited a moment before I spoke.

'Well,' I said at last, after an interval during which she had been watching me narrowly. 'And what makes you think it's a woman?'

'The parcel!' she answered. 'Just that!'

'The parcel, eh? That he fastened on his bicycle?'

'Of course!'

'Well, what about the parcel?'

'The parcel, without a doubt, contained books. I bet anything the books were novels. Who should he be taking novels to but a woman?'

'Good idea, Audrey! You're sure it was books?'

'I handled the parcel. There was only a thin wrapping of brown paper round it. Of course I know the feel of books.'

'Dick had given out that he was going to Verrill's, hadn't he, Audrey?'

'Yes—but that was a lie. Small one, of course, but still a lie. He never had any idea of going to Verrill's. He was going to see some woman. The books were for her. What do you think?'

'I think—now I come to think of it—that it's very probable you're right. But again—what woman? I've never heard of Dick's name being linked with that of any woman hereabouts.'

'It mightn't be hereabouts. He went out of our place at six o'clock, and nobody seems to have seen him anywhere until ten, when he was seen to enter Hagsdene Wood. Well, you can go a long way on a bicycle—and back from wherever you went—in four hours. I can, anyway!'

I had to think a bit over that. Then I remembered something.

'Yes,' I said. 'But look here, Audrey—those two young people who saw Dick enter the wood say that he had the parcel on his machine then. What do you make of that?'

'I make this—which is a common-sense deduction. He took the books somewhere, to somebody. He brought back other books from that somebody which he'd lent her before.'

But I shook my head at that.

'Scarcely, Audrey! If he did—if you're right—why did he take the parcel off his machine when he went into the wood? Why should he carry a parcel of returned books—we'll suppose they were to be returned to a library—into the wood with him?'

'Ah, but I've got you there!' she retorted, triumphantly. 'He was going somewhere for the night, and he took the parcel with him, knowing that if he left it on his bicycle all night in the wood the books would get damp! That's why!'

'Very clever, very ingenious,' I said. 'But how do you know he left his bicycle all night in the wood?'

'I'm sure he did,' she replied. 'I saw it next day. There was rust on it, and the saddle was damp. There was rain during that night. Of course he left it in the wood—while he went elsewhere.'

'Yes—and where?' I said. 'Where? If we only knew that!'

'Can't you find out? Aren't you doing anything to find out?'

'I'm going to do all I can to find out. Listen, Audrey! Do you think Dick's shielding the murderer—or somebody else?'

'Somebody else! A woman. I don't think it's anything to do with the murderer at all. I'm certain he was taking those books to a woman. He doesn't want it to be known what woman.'

'You've no idea yourself?'

'None! Not the remotest! But I think you should find out where he got those books and what they were, and if he'd been in the habit of buying or borrowing books. Can't you?'

'I can and will! I'll make a note of that, Audrey. It's worth following up.'

'Yes—and then there's the stick!'

'What about the stick?'

'The stick that was found in the wood, with which they suggest Maidment was struck down. That fellow Hebb, who in my opinion is a sneaking hound, swears that he gave it to Dick. That's rot! He did give Dick a stick, of the same sort, a cheap, common oak stick. But one oak stick is as like another as two peas—how could he swear that was the same stick? Besides, I know jolly well that that is not the stick which Dick fastened on his bicycle that evening as he was making ready to leave the house!'

I pricked up my ears at that.

'You do, eh?' I exclaimed. 'Certain?'

'Dead certain! The stick that Dick fastened on his machine was an ash-plant.'

'Good! I'll make a note of that too. Dick always carried a stick, didn't he? Wherever he went, eh?'

'Always! Habit of his, ever since he was a mere boy.'

'Come to think of it,' I remarked, 'I never remember seeing Dick without one. So it wasn't an oak stick, but an ash-plant?'

'It was an ash-plant!'

'You'd swear to that?'

'Till I'm black in the face! Do you think I can't trust my own eyes?'

'Nobody better, I should say, Audrey. Well—but what about this supposed woman? Can't you think of anybody, any woman?'

'I can't! Of course, it's a secret business. Dick's been having an affair with some woman and they've managed to keep it dark.'

'You think that's why he's holding his tongue—so that the woman's name won't come out?'

'Of course! Dick's got some very good points, you know, Ernest. He's not the sort who'd ever give a woman away.'

My thoughts went back to the anonymous typewritten letter handed to me by Mr Wrenne. I gave Audrey a speculative glance.

'Can you keep a secret?' I asked politely.

She returned my glance of speculation by one of scorn.

'I am a woman!' she said, emphasizing the personal pronoun. 'So——'

'A professional secret?' I added.

'Any sort of secret,' she replied. 'If it's necessary!'

'Very well,' I said, finding and handing over the anonymous letter. 'Look at that!'

She took the letter, read it over, once—twice—and laid it down.

'That's a woman's!' she said, with decision. '*The* woman! Where did it come from?'

'It was posted in London,' I answered.

She reflected a while on that.

'I suppose it would be quite easy for anybody to send a letter from Ullathwaite to somebody in London who would post it there?' she said.

'Quite easy! But this letter needn't have been written in Ullathwaite. The sender may have gone from Ullathwaite to London.'

'What're you going to do with it?' she asked.

'Nothing at present. If we could find out who the anonymous writer is it would help. But there's no clue. So I'll turn my immediate attention to the two matters you've mentioned, Audrey—the books and the stick. Now before you go, just think again. Have you ever heard anything, anything at all, which suggests Dick's being mixed up with any love-business?—for that's what it really comes to!'

'But I haven't!' she declared, emphatically. 'We—that is, the family—always regarded Dick as being indifferent to girls. I've never known him show any attention to girls—certainly he's never shown any to any of the girls I know. We've always thought of him as being wrapped up in cricket, and football, and games—he's never been known to run after girls.'

'Ah!' I said. 'That makes it all the worse! If he has had an affair with some lady in secret, he'll have had a bad attack! I'm afraid it's as you say, Audrey—there's a woman in it. Well, we must do what we can to make up for the silence he's evidently determined to keep.'

She went away, and I set to work at once to elucidate the mysteries, such as they were, of the parcel and the stick. And I had no difficulty at all in doing so. The railway-station bookstall manager told me that for some time past Dick Radford had been in the habit of occasionally buying new novels from him, and that he had bought three, previously ordered, on the afternoon of October 17. As to the stick, Shillaker, a tobacconist of the town, who also sold umbrellas and walking-sticks, shown—by Henderson's courtesy—the stick found in the wood, said contemptuously that it was such a common type of article that no man in his senses would swear that it was any identifiable stick. I cheered up a good deal at that: I saw a chance. But—the woman? Was there a woman?

It was just then that I had a brain-wave. I suddenly remembered Jos Harlesworth.

5

Jos (originally known in some far-off times of infancy as Josiah) Harlesworth was a human ferret. His ingenuity in finding things out about people (*i.e.*, his fellow-townsfolk) far exceeded anything that could have been accomplished by an ordinary Paul Pry, and what he did not know about the character, morals, and financial affairs of Ullathwaite people was not worth knowing. Originally a clerk (not articled) to a solicitor of the town, he was now, at something over middle age, a sort of odd-job man. He was always ready to serve a writ or a summons, and he could find a defaulting debtor where process-servers and bailiffs had utterly failed. No Tradesmen's Protection Society knew half as much about the trustworthiness of individuals and families as he did; he could tell grocer, butcher, and baker anything they wanted to know as to the extent of credit that should be given to Smith or Brown or Robinson: I dare say that if it had come to it he could have given very near estimates of balances in the various banks. And he looked the part—a lean, cadaverous person, sharp-nosed, gimlet-eyed, invariably clothed in a tightly buttoned old coat which had become green with age, quick and stealthy-footed, Josiah looked what he was—a human sleuth.

It struck me, on thinking things over after Audrey Radford had left my office, that Jos Harlesworth might be very useful. And, having a very good idea where he could be found at that time of the day, namely, in a certain bar-parlour not far from my office, I sent round for him. Presently he came, accompanied by an aroma of rum flavoured with lemon. It was not his way to greet anyone formally, and he sat down in silence and looked his inquiry as to why he was summoned.

'I want a bit of private talk with you, Jos,' I said familiarly (it was no use being anything but familiar with him) and with a wink which I meant to be knowing. 'Strictly between ourselves, you know.'

'*Entre nous*—as the Frenchmen say, Mr Wilsborough,' he responded quickly. 'I understand, sir. And—as it says in the Latin tongue—*sub rosa.*'

'Very much so,' I assented. 'So let's confine ourselves to plain English. You're pretty well acquainted with the doings of Ullathwaite people, aren't you?'

'I keep my eyes open, Mr Wilsborough,' he answered. 'And my ears! Human nature, sir, is worth serious study.'

'Let's get to business,' I continued. 'You've no objection to earning a nice little fee, I suppose?'

'None whatever, Mr Wilsborough. Money, sir, is always useful—especially to a soldier of fortune.'

'Well, you know all about this Maidment case?'

'No, sir, I do not! If I did——'

'I mean you know what everybody else knows?'

'I know what I heard at the magisterial proceedings, Mr Wilsborough—and at the coroner's inquest.'

'Nothing more?'

'Nothing more, sir. Do not credit me with knowledge which I don't possess!'

'All right! We start out from the beginning, then. Do you know anything about young Dick Radford's private affairs?'

'No, sir, I don't.'

'Ever heard of him in connexion with the fair sex, now?'

'No, sir!'

'No lady of the neighbourhood?'

'No, sir—either married or single.'

'No barmaids, for instance?'

'No, sir. Nor pretty parlourmaids. Nor nursemaids. Nor governesses. Nor shopgirls. As far as my knowledge goes, sir, the young gentleman was not born under the influence of Venus.'

'I suppose you'd have heard if he had been given to—shall we call it philandering, eh?'

'I think I should, Mr Wilsborough. This is a limited community.'

'And you never have heard——'

'Never heard anything of that sort, sir. All I know of Mr Richard Radford is that he's a bit rackety in the way of a fondness for horses, dogs, billiards, sport—loves that sort of thing better than his father's office, you know. But as regards running after the ladies—no!'

I relapsed into silence, wondering how far I had better take Jos Harlesworth into my confidence. He too kept silence, his beady eyes fixed steadily on mine. I suppose we were studying each other. He spoke first.

'May I ask, sir, what all this is about? We are speaking in strict confidence!'

'You may!' I answered, making up my mind. 'You're aware that Dick Radford absolutely refuses to speak—refuses to explain his whereabouts on the night of October 17?'

'I am, sir!'

'He has a reason, of course, for his reticence.'

'Undoubtedly!'

'I think the reason is a woman.'

'I shouldn't wonder, sir. The reason, generally, is a woman. *Cherchez la femme!*—so the Frenchmen say. There is a great deal of truth in it.'

'Well, I want to seek for and find this woman. I think Master Dick was in her company that night.'

'Very likely, sir. May I ask if you have any idea as to the identity of the particular lady?'

'You may! I haven't. That's just it.'

'Nor of her—shall we call it locality? Whereabouts?'

'I think we'll go back to the evidence,' I said. 'Dick Radford was seen to enter Hagsdene Wood at ten o'clock on the night of October 17 by two credible witnesses. After concealing his bicycle among some bushes, he took from it a parcel, believed to contain books—three novels, in fact—and a stick, and went across the wood in the direction of Hebb's cottage. Now he certainly did not go to Hebb's place—they saw nothing of him. But there is a path near there which leads across a field or two to those better-class houses——'

'Down in the valley, sir,' he interrupted. 'I know them well. Also their tenants—owners or occupiers. Mr Garland, Mr Pratt, Colonel Wharton, Mr Walkingham, Mr Norrington. Five!'

'Well, beyond those five houses there is nothing but open country. We think it likely that Dick Radford went to one of those houses—spent the night there, concealed. Now, is there any lady——?'

Jos Harlesworth pulled me up with a sharp exclamation.

'Ah!' he said. 'Ah! Now . . . let me think a moment. Ah! Um!'

He took his sharply angled chin in his hand and thought for a minute or two. Then he turned to me with a sly expression in his eyes.

'Ah, just so!' he said. 'Now I wonder——'

'Well?' I asked as he hesitated. 'You wonder——?'

'Mr Norrington, sir, is an elderly gentleman, a semi-invalid. But he has a very young and very pretty wife——'

'I've seen her,' I said. 'Though I don't know her personally.'

'Pretty—and young,' he went on. 'When I say young, I mean she's young compared to her husband. Mr Norrington, sir, is, I should say, seventy years of age: Mrs Norrington is on the right side of thirty. It is said, sir, that she was a nurse—and that Mr Norrington married her so that she could nurse him. Very attractive woman, sir, and has talents beyond those of the nursing art. She took a share in the labours of our local dramatic society last winter and acquitted herself with credit.'

'I remember—but I didn't see her performance,' I said. 'Well?'

'Well, sir, the only lady—really, *the* only lady—I can think of in that neighbourhood who would be likely to attract any young man is young Mrs Norrington—all the rest of the ladies there, in those five houses, are either frumps or frights. But I have never heard Mrs Norrington's name coupled with that of young Radford, nor with anyone's.'

'There is such a thing as secrecy,' I remarked. 'Let me see—is Dick Radford a member of that amateur dramatic society?'

'He is, sir. He had a minor, a very minor, part in the performance in which Mrs Norrington had one of the principal ones.'

That made me think a bit. And again Josiah Harlesworth and I watched each other.

'I wonder if Mrs Norrington is the lady?' I said at last.

He moved his head slowly from one side to the other.

'There would be nothing surprising in the fact, if she was, sir,' he remarked. 'Mr Norrington is, as I have said, an elderly man and an invalid, and she is young, pretty, and lively. And young Radford is a good-looking lad.'

'But their names have never been connected,' I said.

'As far as I am aware—no,' he answered. 'But my knowledge, Mr Wilsborough, is—not infinite.'

'Still,' I said, 'I dare say you could find out, Josiah?'

'If there is anything to find out, sir, I can find it,' he replied quietly. 'You may depend on me for that. I suppose I may have what the French call *carte blanche* in the way of—er, expenses?'

I knew what he meant and I gave him a cheque for what I considered a reasonable amount.

'You'll be careful,' I said as he rose to go.

'Where the reputation of a lady is at stake, sir, I am something more than careful,' he replied. 'I shall be most guarded—and no one but you will hear what I have—or, rather, may have—to tell. If there is a secret, sir, and I unearth it, I may say this—it will not be the first I have unearthed!'

6

When Josiah Harlesworth had gone away I gave myself up to a few minutes' serious reflection on the matter we had been discussing. Was there what people call 'something' between Mrs Norrington and

Dick Radford, and was that the reason for his attitude of determined silence? The more I thought of it, the more I felt it to be highly probable. Mrs Norrington, as far as I knew anything about her, was young, pretty, vivacious; her husband was a semi-invalid, twice her age; Dick Radford was a good-looking young fellow—the very sort to catch a woman's eye and stir her fancy. It might be so—and if it were so, it would explain his refusal to speak. It would also explain his doings on the night of October 17. But how were we going to get at the truth? Two people knew it (that is, if there was anything to know); one was Dick, the other the lady. Dick, I felt sure, would not open his lips, even if he died for it; no one could expect her to open hers. Still . . . the anonymous letter! The writer of that had made an explicit statement—nay, there were two statements:

> From a quarter past ten onwards Richard Radford was not near the scene of the murder, though he probably passed it a few minutes after ten o'clock on his way elsewhere.

On his way elsewhere! But where? Being now very familiar with what I may call the geography of the affair, I knew that Richard Radford could have walked from the place where Ellen Hopkinson and James Collier saw him, at the entrance to the wood, through the wood, past Hebb's cottage, across the meadow beneath the wood, to Mr Norrington's house in the valley, in just under ten minutes. Did he go to that house—to keep an appointment, an assignation, call it whatever you like, with Mrs Norrington? *Did* he? But there was the further explicit statement:

> If the worst comes to the worst Richard Radford's innocence of either murder or robbery can, and will be, proved to the full.

Now what did that mean? Surely just this: that there was somebody—who could it be but the writer of the letter?—who knew where Dick Radford was from 10.15 that night, and, if he were found guilty, would come forward to prove his whereabouts. Was that somebody Mrs Norrington? If so, it meant just this—that Mrs Norrington would have to say, disregarding any consequences, that Dick Radford spent the night of October 17, from a quarter past ten onward, in her company!—or, if not absolutely in her company, then, at any rate, somewhere within her absolute knowledge.

Arrived at this stage of reflection, I wondered—but not for

long—if it would do any good if I went to see Dick and plumped him straight out with two or three direct questions? I very soon decided not to do anything of the sort. Dick was in a very ugly mood, and I felt sure that if I even mentioned Mrs Norrington's name he would be furiously angry. Moreover, up to then it was all guesswork, and wouldn't help in solving the mystery of the murder or give me a clue to the identity of the real murderer. I determined to wait; to do nothing until I got a report from my ferret, Josiah.

Josiah worked as swiftly as secretly. Within four days he came to me with a knowing look in his eyes.

'Well?' I said as he sat down by my desk. 'Any luck?'

'A modicum, sir, a modicum!' he replied. 'It does not bulk largely, Mr Wilsborough, but—as one would say if one expressed one's self in the Latin language—it may be *multum in parvo*, sir.'

'What is it, anyway?' I asked.

'Just this, sir,' he answered, settling himself for a confidential talk. 'My practical experience, Mr Wilsborough, has taught me that if one wishes to become acquainted with what one may term family or private history—that is to say, the intimate doings, concerns, affairs, loves, hates, and so on of a household—one should cultivate the acquaintance of the—er, domestics.'

'Cooks, parlourmaids, housemaids, eh?' I said. 'Well?'

'I have acquired deeply valuable information from a scullery-maid before to-day, sir,' he answered, calmly. 'In this case, however, it is a parlourmaid.'

'Mrs——'

He held up a finger, and glanced at the door.

'I don't think we should mention names, sir,' he said. 'The matter grows serious—in my opinion. Shall we say Mrs X? X, I believe, signifies——'

'Go on, Josiah,' I said. 'Mrs—the lady in question—isn't an unknown quantity—we know who she is. But call her Mrs X. Mrs X's parlourmaid, then? What about her? And who is she?'

'The X family—small, sir, husband and wife only—are away from home, and for some time. The domestic staff—cook, parlourmaid, housemaid, page-boy—remain at home, on board wages. I have made the acquaintance of the parlourmaid, sir.'

'Profitably?' I inquired.

He held up a hand to his lips and coughed, discreetly.

'A cautious woman, sir,' he answered. 'She——'

'What's her name?' I interrupted.

'Louisa Gibbs, sir. Louisa——'

'Oh, I know Louisa Gibbs!' I interrupted again. 'She used to be in my mother's employ.'

'Precisely, sir. That is what I am coming to. Louisa, sir, is a cautious person. She will not confide in me.'

'Got nothing out of her, then, eh?' I said.

'I, personally, no, sir—at least, no more than an admission that she can tell something if she likes. I will repeat Louisa's exact words, Mr Wilsborough. "I won't say one word to you, Josiah!" she said. "You're a regular Nosey Parker," she said. "And I don't trust Nosey Parkers. But," she continued, "I'll talk to Master Ernest willingly," she said. Meaning you, sir.'

'Oh, Louisa will talk to me, will she?' I said. 'Very good, Josiah. When?'

'Louisa, sir, would prefer to call upon you when you are quite alone,' he replied. 'She wishes her visit and her communication to be absolutely *sub rosa*—as they say in the Latin tongue.'

'Bring her here at six o'clock this evening, then,' I answered. 'And tell her that our talk will be strictly—as they say in French, Josiah—*entre nous*. Got that?'

'I have it, sir. The lady shall attend you at precisely six o'clock. You will require my attendance?'

'I think you'd better be somewhere about,' I answered. 'Come with her, anyhow.'

Louisa Gibbs, with Josiah in attendance, presented herself in my private room at the hour appointed. All my clerks had gone; I installed Josiah in their office and gave him *The Times* and a cigar wherewith to amuse himself: Louisa I conducted into my sanctum. I knew Louisa well enough; she was old enough to be my mother, and had been my mother's parlourmaid for several years when I was in my infancy: consequently we were on familiar terms.

'Well, Louisa,' I said, when I had given her the easiest chair in the place. 'So you've got something to tell me?'

Louisa looked at the door which shut off Josiah.

'I wasn't going to tell him, you know, Master Ernest,' she said. 'At any rate, not when I could tell you. Better master than man!—that's what I say.'

'But you can tell something?' I asked.

She pointed a long forefinger at the door.

'He's been at me, this last day or two, to find out if I know anything about my mistress and young Radford,' she answered. 'Of course, I shouldn't say—to him!'

'But do you?' I said.

'Well, you tell me something, Master Ernest,' she replied. 'Is that young fellow in real danger?'

'You may take it that he is, Louisa. Yes!'

'Will it help him if I tell you what I do know?' she asked.

'Probably! He's shielding somebody, and I have an idea it may be Mrs Norrington. I think he may have been with Mrs Norrington on the night of October 17. If he was——'

She shook her head at that.

'Well, I don't know how that could be,' she said. 'Mrs Norrington was not at home that night. But I'd better tell you what I do know, Master Ernest. And let me tell you this, too. What I'm going to tell you I've never told to any other living soul! If your poor mother was alive, she'd tell you that Louisa Gibbs is no tale-bearer and never was.'

'I'm quite sure of it, Louisa,' I hastened to say. 'And that'll make your evidence all the more valuable.'

'I don't know about its being evidence,' she said. 'I'm no hand at the law, of course. It's just what I've seen. You know, Master Ernest, that Mrs Norrington is a very pretty and lively lady, and a good five-and-thirty years younger than her husband, and he's only a poor invalid, full of fads—I reckon she'd never have married him but for his money. Well, it's dull for her there—no denying of it. She did get a bit of relaxation when she took part in those theatricals last winter, to be sure. And it was not so long after that, perhaps two or three weeks after, that I saw something that made me suspect there might be something between her and young Mr Radford.'

'Yes—and what was it, Louisa?' I asked.

'Well, it happened to be my weekly day off, Master Ernest, and I went over to Grandminster to do a bit of shopping. And as I was sauntering down the High Street I saw Mrs Norrington and young Radford together. They were coming out of the Northern Provinces Hotel—you know what a grand place that is. That was just about half-past two in the afternoon; I supposed they'd been having lunch there. They didn't see me, though I was close by. And, of course, it made me think—and wonder.'

'Anything else, Louisa?' I asked. 'Ever seen them together on any other occasion?'

'Yes—once!' she replied. 'Just once. You don't know Mr Norrington's place, Master Ernest?—the house and grounds, I mean.'

'Not at all, Louisa! Never been there.'

'Well, you know,' she continued, 'the garden and grounds, at the back of the house, go down to the stream that runs through that valley—you can scarcely call it a river. There's a little bridge over that stream that leads into Mr Norrington's grounds, and near the bridge there's a summer-house that Mr Norrington had built when he bought the place, and fitted up very comfortable, like a sitting-room with easy chairs and sofas and such like things. Well, late one night this last summer—July, it would be—I went down our kitchen-garden for a bit of a walk—it was a very hot, stifling night—and as the kitchen-garden's at the back of the summer-house I had to pass it. And I distinctly heard Mrs Norrington's voice in there—she was laughing, and I know her laugh among a thousand. Laughing as if—well, as if she was trying to keep from laughing, you understand. And of course I wondered what she was doing in there at that time, for it was somewhere about ten o'clock. And we're all curious, you know, Master Ernest, so I just got where I could watch the door, and after a while I saw the mistress and young Radford come out. She went off to the house, and he crossed the bridge and went up the meadow at the other side of the stream; there's a path there that leads past Hebb's cottage into Hagsdene Wood. And—that's all.'

'You saw both your mistress and young Radford, Louisa? Clearly?'

'As clear as I see you! And for a good reason. There was a strong light in our kitchen window and when they came out of the summer-house, it shone full on them. Oh, yes, I saw them clearly!—I shouldn't say I did if I hadn't.'

'Did you never see anything of that sort again?'

'Never! But I've known of the mistress going down the garden late at night, and I'd my own notions as to why.'

I thought over this information for a while. Then:

'Look here, Louisa,' I said. 'I said to you just now that I had a suspicion that young Radford may have been in Mrs Norrington's company on the night of October 17, and you replied that you didn't know how that could be because she wasn't at home that night. Where was she, then?'

'At Harrogate, Master Ernest. Mr and Mrs Norrington went to the United Empire Hotel at Harrogate on the 2nd October, and they were there, to my knowledge, until the 23rd.'

'What about the house—here?' I asked.

'The house was closed, Master Ernest. There was no one in it. Just as there's no one in it now. It's closed for the winter.'

'Where are Mr and Mrs Norrington, then?'

'Gone to Egypt, until the end of March. Then they're going to Italy, and they'll come home about the beginning of May. He always spends his winters abroad.'

'Do you know,' I asked, 'if they went straight from Harrogate to Egypt?'

'I know that they left Harrogate for London first,' she answered. 'I had one or two letters from Mrs Norrington written from London. She said in the last one that they were just about leaving for Egypt.'

'Did she give you any address in Egypt?' I asked.

'Yes. Shepheard's Hotel, Cairo.'

'I suppose she didn't make any reference to this murder affair, Louisa?'

'No, Master Ernest, she didn't. But I'll tell you what she did. She asked me to post her the local papers regularly.'

'Did you think that at all strange?'

'Well, I did! For this reason: I never knew Mrs Norrington to read the local paper before—nor Mr Norrington either. It certainly never came into the house, unless some of us servants bought it. Mr Norrington he had *The Times* regular; she read the *Morning Post*. I remember her once picking up the local paper in the servants' hall and making some remark about two-headed lambs and giant cucumbers—a scornful remark, like. A very high-and-mighty young lady, you know, Mrs Norrington is!—though they do say she was nothing but a nurse when he married her.'

It seemed to me that there was no more information than this to be got out of Louisa Gibbs, and after cautioning her to say nothing to anyone but myself I brought our interview to an end. And when she was gone I reckoned things up. I had been working on the supposition that Dick Radford was in the company of Mrs Norrington on the night of October 17 and that he was keeping silence because he could not betray her. But that theory fell clear to the ground if Mrs Norrington on that night was at the United Empire Hotel at Harrogate. But—here came in another 'but'—*was* she? *Was* she at Harrogate that night? Or—unknown to anyone but Dick—*was she at home*?

7

I may as well say, at this stage, that from the first moment in which the matter had been placed in my hands I had felt a profound belief in Dick Radford's innocence of the charge brought against him. True, there was some very ugly evidence to get over. And in addition to the evidence there was a baffling mystery about the whole thing which I saw no prospect of solving. Somebody killed and robbed Roger Maidment—but *who*? One thing I felt convinced of—Dick Radford was not shielding the murderer. But he was undoubtedly shielding some other person. And on the evidence just acquired from Louisa Gibbs I felt sure that that reason was Mrs Norrington. I figured things up like this: There was some sort of an intrigue, a liaison, call it what you like, between Mrs Norrington and Dick. What was to prevent Mrs Norrington making some excuse to her husband, coming over from their hotel at Harrogate, and staying the night in her own house at Ullathwaite, having previously arranged with Dick to meet her there? It was sheer coincidence, nothing less, that that night of October 17 should be the very night on which Maidment was murdered. But there was no doubt—the medical evidence and other evidence proved it—that Maidment could not have been murdered before ten-thirty or ten-forty-five on that night. Now if, by Mrs Norrington's evidence, I could prove that Dick Radford met her at a quarter past ten and was with her from that time until early next morning the whole case against him would fall through. To be sure, there was the question of the perforated sovereign. But I was going to contend that it was simply ridiculous to suggest that the perforated sovereign handed by Dick to Fardale on the morning of the 18th was the very same coin given by Collingwood to Maidment. Sovereigns with small holes drilled through them, if not as thick as blackberries, were at least fairly numerous—it was by no means an uncommon thing for men to attach perforated sovereigns as pendants to watch-chains. I could not believe that any jury would hang Dick Radford on merely that bit of evidence; that Collingwood handed Maidment a sovereign with a hole in it, and that Dick gave Fardale another, similarly disfigured, was just—coincidence. I meant to rely a good deal on that for my defence, but I knew that if I could establish an alibi, through Mrs Norrington's evidence, I should be far safer. And—keeping everything to myself meanwhile, not letting Dick, nor his father, nor anybody else know what I was after—I meant to *make* Mrs Norrington speak! That is, to make her speak if I could only get a hold on her.

To do that, it was necessary to do a little detective work myself. I could not entrust this job to Josiah Harlesworth. To do him justice, Josiah did not attempt to get out of me anything imparted by Louisa Gibbs. Beyond a polite expression of hope that my interview with Louisa had not been unprofitable, Josiah asked nothing. I gave him some further work on which to exercise his ferret-like capacities, and resolving to be my own sleuth went off at the week-end to the United Empire Hotel at Harrogate to find out as much as I could about Mrs Norrington's doings and movements on the 17th October.

I began by cultivating the acquaintance of the Manager of the hotel, a retired officer of the Royal Navy, and by the second day of my stay I had formed the opinion that I might safely take him into my entire confidence. I did so. As soon as I mentioned Mrs Norrington's name I saw that he was quite well acquainted with her.

'Mr and Mrs Norrington,' he said, 'are regular visitors here. They have come here for the last three or four years, usually twice a year, sometimes oftener. They were last here in October. They came, as far as I remember, about the beginning of October and stayed until nearly the end of the month. Then they left for London on their way, I understood, to Egypt for the winter. What is it, now, that you particularly want to know?'

'I want to know where Mrs Norrington was on the night of October 17?' I replied. 'Just exactly that!'

'As far as I can trust my memory she was here,' he answered. 'I don't remember that she ever went away for a night. October 17? That date seems familiar. Wait a minute,' he continued, opening a diary that lay on his desk. 'October 17, eh? Ah, yes, we had a ball here that night. I don't think Mrs Norrington would miss that: Mrs Norrington was very fond of dancing.'

'Is there any way of making absolutely sure?' I asked.

'I can make dead certain,' he replied. 'We have here a Mrs Carstairs, a widow lady, still young, who is a permanent resident. Mrs Carstairs interests herself greatly in all our social events—balls, dances, concerts, all that sort of thing. Mrs Carstairs is, moreover, a close friend of Mrs Norrington. She will be able to say definitely if Mrs Norrington was here that night.'

'I don't want Mrs Norrington to get wind of my inquiries,' I said. 'Is Mrs Carstairs——?'

'Oh, leave that to me!' he said. 'If you like to see me again in an hour or two I'll see Mrs Carstairs in the meantime, and I'll get you absolutely accurate information. Mrs Carstairs will remember October 17 clearly, because that ball, I see, was the first of our present series, and she was very keen about making it a success: I remember, now I come to think of it, that she and Mrs Norrington worked very hard to ensure its success. And—you see how I'm brushing up my memory—I'm sure that Mrs Norrington was at the ball that night, because I remember dancing with her!'

'That seems to settle matters!' I said, disappointedly. 'Doesn't it?'

'All the same, I'll see Mrs Carstairs,' he replied. 'Look in again, Mr Wilsborough, before dinner to-night.'

I looked in again, just before going to my room to dress. At sight of me the Manager shook his head.

'Well, my dear sir,' he said. 'I have ascertained three positive facts for you—absolute facts! There is no doubt whatever about them. On October 17 last Mrs Norrington lunched here with Mrs Carstairs. She spent the afternoon with Mrs Carstairs completing arrangements for the ball that evening. She dined with Mrs Carstairs before the ball. She was at the ball, in our ballroom, from the first dance, at 9.30, to the last at two o'clock in the morning. And she certainly slept here. So there you are! Oh, of course, Mr Wilsborough, this is all strictly between ourselves—absolutely so!'

So my attempt to establish an alibi through Mrs Norrington's evidence came to an inglorious end! I finished my week-end at Harrogate and went home to Ullathwaite still pondering over the problem—where was Dick Radford on the night of October 17. And why wouldn't he tell?

8

I had not said a word to Mr Radford senior about all this, and now, finding that Mrs Norrington had certainly not left the United Empire Hotel at Harrogate on the evening and night of October 17, I determined not to do so. But on my return to Ullathwaite, after concluding my inquiries at Harrogate, I went to see Mr Radford.

Mr Radford was difficult to make out. I could not understand him. Some people might have thought him absolutely apathetic, even indifferent. Others might have stamped him as a confirmed fatalist. It seemed as if he had said to himself: 'This unfortunate thing has come about; I cannot do anything; it must take its course.' And when I called on him his tone was listless.

'Anything new, Wilsborough?' he asked in a dull voice.

'Nothing!' I replied. 'But I want to ask you a question. Please give me a plain answer—I'm sure it will be truthful. Do you know where your son was on the night of October 17?'

He stared at me in genuine surprise.

'I?' he exclaimed. 'I? Indeed I do not!'

'You've no idea, suspicion?'

'Neither!' he replied. 'Neither!'

'Do you think your wife knows? Or your daughter?'

'I am as certain that they do not as I am certain that I do not,' he answered. 'Certain! They know nothing. None of us know anything of his movements or doings from the time he left the house that evening.'

'Do you think, Mr Radford, that Dick had some secret affair with—we'd better be plain—somebody in the town or neighbourhood? Lady—woman—girl—anybody of the other sex?'

'I've no grounds for thinking such a thing,' he answered.

'Who was it, then, that he was taking the novels to?' I suggested.

'I have no idea. But it need not necessarily have been a woman. He had friends of his own sex.'

'Any friend of his own sex would have come forward,' I said. 'As it is, we're left with the fact that he utterly refuses to explain his movements and his acquisition of that perforated sovereign. It's a trying situation, Mr Radford—and a dangerous one.'

I was watching him closely, but I could not detect any sign of emotion or anxiety in his expression.

'You've secured Henshawe?' he asked, after a brief silence.

'I have!'

'Henshawe ought to secure a verdict,' he remarked quietly. 'I confidently expect that he will.'

'And what do you expect Henshawe to go on, Mr Radford?' I asked. 'He's all the evidence before him now, of course.'

'I expect him to go on this,' he answered. 'There are three points, at any rate, that I should go on. First of all, no one can prove that the banknotes handed by Dick to Fardale were the banknotes paid by the Hagsdene Park people to Maidment: there's proof that they were not. Secondly, what absolute proof is there that the perforated sovereign given by Dick to Fardale (if he did give it) is the one received by Maidment from Collingwood? Perforated sovereigns are not uncommon; I have one myself at the end of a chain which I never use. And thirdly, the stick found in the wood is not the stick which—I am relying on my daughter's evidence—which Dick strapped on his bicycle when he left home that night. In Henshawe's hands all this should be driven home!'

'Henshawe will strain every nerve to get a verdict, Mr Radford,' I said. 'But things would be simplified if Dick would speak.'

He shook his head slowly and gravely.

'I do not think Dick will speak, under any compulsion,' he said.

'But I feel sure that he will not be found guilty!'

'Juries are queer things to deal with,' I remarked. 'You know that yourself! Still, we've got the right man in Henshawe.'

Henshawe, Q.C., was the most likely man then practising in the criminal courts for this particular case, and he had won for himself a great reputation for his work before North Country juries. He was something of a character—a very tall, broadly built man, with the head and shoulders of a giant, a roaring voice, and, I am afraid, a good deal of a bullying manner. He was given to browbeating witnesses—and to occasional differences with judges—but his record showed that he was highly successful in defence, and he himself in his humorous moments was not above boasting that he had restored many a criminal to his friends and relations. I felt that if anybody could get Dick Radford off it was Henshawe.

Henshawe, just before the Grandminster Assizes came on, went with me to see Dick. He looked him carefully over before speaking to him. Then he opened on Dick in characteristic fashion.

'Well, young fellow!' he said, almost truculently. 'Do you know that you're running your precious neck into a noose?'

Dick gave him back look for look.

'Am I?' he said coolly.

'Not a doubt of it!—unless you come to your senses. Now then, don't be a damned young idiot any longer! Out with it, and be done with it! Tell me and your solicitor all about it!'

'All about what?' asked Dick with an assumption of infinite innocence.

'All about where you were that night! Come on, now! Who is it you're shielding?'

'Who said I was shielding anybody?' retorted Dick.

'Of course you are! Now then, where were you that night?'

'No!' said Dick.

Henshawe stared at him. Dick stared back.

'Supposing I throw up my brief?' demanded Henshawe.

'I never employed you,' replied Dick.

'No, but your dad did, my boy, and at a nice cost to his pocket, too!' said Henshawe. 'Now are you going to help?'

'Not in the way you indicate!' answered Dick.

'Damn you for as silly a young ass as ever I saw!' exclaimed Henshawe. 'Well, will you tell me this, then? Did you give six sovereigns to Fardale, the bookmaker?'

'Yes, of course—I've acknowledged it.'

'Did you see a perforated coin among them?'

'No! And I've said that before!'

'If there was one you never noticed it?'

'Certainly I never noticed it.'

'Well, where did you get those sovereigns?'

'No!' said Dick. 'That's another thing I do not tell!'

'Well, tell this, then—hang it all, it's between ourselves, my lad! You saw that stick, an oak stick, they produced before the magistrates—the stick that was found in the wood? You did? Well, was it yours?'

'No!'

'Was it the stick you fastened on your bicycle when you left your father's house that evening?'

'No, it was not. That was an ash-plant.'

'An ash-plant, eh? Um! Where is it now?'

For a moment Dick was off his guard, and I thought he was going to reply. But he checked himself.

'Can't say!' he replied.

'Now then, now then, young fellow, I know what that means!' said Henshawe. 'It means you won't say. Eh?'

'I won't say!' answered Dick.

'But you know? Ah—ah! Very good—then you're going to let me fight with one hand tied behind my back, are you?'

Dick grinned—I am not sure that he didn't wink at his questioner.

'I think you'll tackle 'em, Mr Henshawe,' he said. 'Sorry I can't be of any more assistance to you. But I've said my say!'

9

I don't know what Henshawe thought about this interview with Dick Radford (he was not the sort of man who readily shares his thoughts), but I came away from it more surprised and puzzled than ever. What surprised me was Dick's cocksure confidence; what puzzled me was that he appeared to consider it impossible that anyone could find out anything about his movements on the night of the murder. Once more my thoughts went back to what I considered the critical moment of that night. The evidence of the tenants at Hagsdene Park, and especially of Collingwood, showed beyond doubt that Roger Maidment, however rapidly he had walked (the police, under Superintendent Henderson's personal supervision, had made several tests of distances and time), could not have reached Hagsdene Wood before twenty-five minutes to eleven at the very earliest. Now the anonymous letter stated explicitly that if need arose it could be proved that Dick was elsewhere than in Hagsdene Wood from a quarter past ten. If that was true—and I believed it to be true—Dick Radford was somewhere else, and the writer of the letter knew where. But—who was the writer?

At various times, during the period that elapsed between Dick Radford's last appearance before the magistrates and the opening of the Grandminster Assizes, I had made several careful examinations and inspections of Hagsdene Wood and its immediate surroundings, and had carefully noted down items and calculations about distances, times, and the like. There was no doubt whatever that Dick Radford entered Hagsdene Wood at ten o'clock—the evidence of Ellen Hopkinson and Jim Collier proved that. Well, it wouldn't take him more than five minutes to cross the wood. Had he gone there, it wouldn't have taken him more than another five minutes to cross the meadow beyond the wood and reach the Norringtons' house at its foot. But as Mrs Norrington was not there, why should he have gone there? Did he go there—not knowing that she wasn't at home? I dismissed that—he must have known she was not at home; he would know. What other houses were there, then, in the neighbourhood to which he could have gone? Well, there were three close to the Norringtons'. But we had ascertained, beyond doubt, that he went to none of them. There remained but one place anywhere near the wood—and that was Hebb's cottage. And Hebb and his wife had sworn that they never saw him, heard of him, knew anything about him. The more I examined it, the deeper the mystery grew.

The next thing that happened after Henshawe and I had seen Dick was a call on me by Mrs Radford, his mother. Mrs Radford, heavily veiled, came to see me one evening as I was about to leave the office. She came at that hour, I suppose, because it was already dark in the streets and town and she didn't want to be recognized. When I got her into my private room I saw that she was nervous and frightened.

'Mr Wilsborough,' she said in a low voice, 'I had to come and see you, and I don't want anybody to know I've come, and my husband least of all. Mr Wilsborough, what is being done for that unhappy boy of mine?'

I told her all we had done and explained the difficulties. If Dick could only be induced to speak——

'I don't think anything will make him speak if he doesn't wish it,' she said. 'He has always been obstinate. He is shielding somebody!'

'No doubt!' I agreed.

'Is it—the murderer?' she asked.

'I don't think so, Mrs Radford. My opinion is that in spite of all the circumstantial evidence Dick knows nothing whatever about either murder or robbery. I think he is shielding—somebody else.'

'A woman?' she exclaimed.

'Most probably!'

'In that case he won't speak,' she said. 'He has a strong sense of honour. But, Mr Wilsborough, there's his—life! And there must be somebody who knows where he was that night and who could save him by coming forward!'

'Undoubtedly, Mrs Radford!'

'Perhaps,' she continued, looking anxiously at me, 'perhaps there is more than one person who knows?'

'There may be,' I assented.

'Servants?' she said. 'Who—have been persuaded to hold their tongues?'

'Perhaps,' I agreed. 'That may be, too.'

She sat clasping and unclasping her hands for a while in silence. Then she turned to me again.

'Mr Wilsborough,' she said, 'I don't want my husband to know anything about what I'm going to say to you. I have a little money that no one knows anything about. How would it be if you put out a reward to anyone who can tell us where my son was that night? Some people will do anything for money! Supposing some—servant, eh?—knows that Dick was—somewhere? A substantial reward?'

'What would you suggest, Mrs Radford?' I asked.

She opened an old-fashioned reticule, a thing rarely seen nowadays, even in this later Victorian period, and, drawing out a bulky envelope, laid it on my desk.

'There's a thousand pounds there, Mr Wilsborough,' she said simply. 'Do with it what you will, but try what I have suggested. I must do something—I cannot feel as my husband feels, that things must run their course.'

'Mr Radford believes that there isn't the least doubt of an acquittal,' I remarked. 'He is sure of it.'

'Ah, but I must do something!' she said. 'Do use that money as I suggest. There must be somebody who *knows*!'

I locked the money away in a drawer and turned to her.

'Mrs Radford,' I said, 'be frank with me. Have you any suspicion that your son had had any intrigue, affair, liaison, anything you like to call it, with any of your own sex in the town or neighbourhood? If you have, say!'

She sat for some time in silence. At last she raised her head.

'I've wondered,' she replied. 'I've wondered if—if he hadn't been very much taken by that pretty Mrs Norrington? But——'

'That'll do, Mrs Radford,' I interrupted. 'I too have had certain suspicions. But I have made some inquiry—and Mrs Norrington was not in Ullathwaite on the night of October 17.'

She looked at me in silence for a moment.

'Perhaps so,' she said, slowly. 'Still——'

'Yes?' I said. 'You mean?'

'He may have gone after her,' she continued. 'Where was she?'

'Staying at Harrogate,' I replied.

'Twenty miles away!' she exclaimed. 'What is twenty miles to a young man on a bicycle?'

I thought this over for a minute or two. Why hadn't I thought of it before?

'Very good, Mrs Radford,' I said. 'Leave matters to me. I'll make a big effort in the way you suggest.'

Before noon next day I had spread the news all over the country, by poster, handbill, and advertisement, that a thousand pounds reward would be paid to anyone who could give accurate information as to the whereabouts of Richard Radford on the night of October 17.

This was some days before the opening of the Assizes at Grandminster. When they opened I was still without one single response to my offer. It was only too evident that nobody knew anything.

10

The trial came on at an early stage of the Assize business. It is not necessary that I should give any detailed account of the proceedings. We heard once more the evidence against Dick which had been already given before the Ullathwaite magistrates. Henshawe did his best with the cross-examination of all the witnesses for the prosecution. But he did not shake Collingwood's evidence nor Fardale's, and if he had some success it was over the question of the stick, the parcel, and the banknotes. He referred to his client's silence and suggested that Dick was shielding somebody, and I, personally, felt that this did not go down well with the Judge, a notoriously severe occupant of the judicial bench. In my opinion the Judge's summing-up went against the prisoner: the only thing his lordship said which could be taken as being in Dick's favour was a remark that perforated sovereigns were not at all uncommon. It was a brief summing-up—but the twelve jurymen were a long time in arriving at their verdict. Retiring at three o'clock in the afternoon they did not return into court until nearly seven hours had elapsed. Then came the verdict.

Not Guilty!

11

I saw my client five minutes after his discharge and took him by the arm.

'Dick!' I said. 'Are you ever going to tell the truth about all this?'

He gave me a hard look.

'P'raps!' he answered. 'P'raps, Wilsborough! When half a dozen people are dead!'

III

THE TWELVE GOOD MEN

(*Statement of Mr Septimus Nettleton, Foreman of the Jury*)

Mr P. W. Wrenne, who was chairman of the bench of magistrates which sent Richard Radford for trial at the Grandminster Assizes, charged with the murder of Roger Maidment at Ullathwaite in October 1899, has asked me—I having been foreman of the jury sworn on that occasion—to set down (in strict confidence) my recollections of the trial. Mr Wrenne, I fancy, is something of a psychologist, and he wants—to put it plainly—something more than mere recollections. Indeed, he specifies what he wants. He asks me to particularize on certain points. In effect, he asks me to answer these questions:

1. What happened after we of the jury retired to consider our verdict?
2. Were there serious differences of opinion among us?
3. If so, how did we eventually arrive at a verdict?

I suppose I ought not to divulge the secrets of a jury, but Mr Wrenne assures me that whatever I tell him will be for his ear alone. I therefore proceed to write down a plain and unvarnished account of what took place between me and my eleven fellow-jurymen after we had been given in charge, locked up, and told to find a verdict.

But, as a preliminary, I wish to make one or two observations. It is a sort of understood thing—judges are very fond of referring to it—that members of a jury know, or ought to know, or can know, nothing whatever about a case until it is put before them in court, or, at any rate, if they do, should dismiss from their minds whatever knowledge they have acquired by reading or hearsay. That is a somewhat difficult if not wholly impossible thing. In this particular case of Regina *v.* Radford I and every one of my fellow-jurymen knew everything possible to be known before ever the case was called. There was practically nothing brought forward at the Assizes which had not already been put before both magistrates and coroner. And as the twelve of us were all local men, living within a radius of twenty or thirty miles of Ullathwaite, and as the newspapers had reported the magisterial proceedings and the coroner's inquiry in full, we were fully cognizant of everything. But—as we were judicially counselled and warned—we were to put all that out of our minds, and listen only to the evidence. I am sure we all honestly tried to do as we were told—but, as will be seen in what I am going to write down, it is difficult to forget knowledge already acquired, and still more difficult to throw aside impressions and convictions gained from it.

2

> 'You shall well and truly try and true deliverance make between our Sovereign Lady the Queen and the prisoner at the bar whom you shall have in charge and a true verdict given according to the evidence. So help you God!'

When the twelfth of us had pledged himself in these solemn words, we settled down—two rows of us, six in a row—in the hard and narrow wooden seats for that purpose provided in the utterly out-of-date and old-fashioned Assize Court of Grandminster. And the first thing we did was to look at the man in the dock whose fate lay in our hands.

Although I live within a few miles of Ullathwaite I had never, as far as I can remember, seen young Richard Radford before. I knew, of course, who he was—the only son of Mr John Radford, a prominent solicitor of Ullathwaite, and at that time Mayor (for a second year of office) of the town. And my first impression of him, as he stood there, self-possessed and of quiet demeanour, in the dock, was that anything less like a murderer, actual or potential, I had never seen. He was just a well-grown, athletic-looking, handsome lad; the sort that women look on with favour and parents with pride. I had no doubt that on occasion he could look sulky, and perhaps ugly, but he showed no sign of sulkiness or anger when he stepped into view before us, and his answer to the charge was given clearly and confidently: there was, indeed, something in the ring of his voice which seemed to indicate that he himself had no doubt as to what our verdict would be. Having pleaded, he began to look round him, studying judge, jurymen, barristers, clerks, officials, and spectators as if they had been so many curiosities set up for his amusement.

But the leading counsel for the prosecution, having expressed a polite wish that his lordship might be pleased—I suppose to allow him to proceed—was already addressing us of the jury. I propose—as Mr Wrenne is already well acquainted with the details—to summarize the story he set forth:

On the evening of October 17 one Roger Maidment, an accountant and rent-collector, of Ullathwaite, in pursuance of a monthly custom went to Hagsdene Park, some way out of the town, to collect certain rents from the tenants of some property there. He collected in all about £110, some of it in cheques, some in banknotes, some in gold. One tenant, Collingwood, paid him in gold, and among the gold was a perforated sovereign—Collingwood called Maidment's attention to it, but Maidment took it. Maidment left Hagsdene Park at a quarter past ten, and went homeward by way of Hagsdene Wood: it would take him twenty minutes at least to reach Hagsdene Wood from Hagsdene Park. Early next morning his dead body was found in Hagsdene Wood by a gamekeeper. He had been killed by one or more blows from some heavy weapon—later a thick, almost bludgeon-like oak walking-stick was discovered hidden close by: in the opinion of the medical men, it was just the sort of thing to cause the injuries which had resulted in death; also, it was their opinion that one of the blows would have been sufficient to kill, and that death had taken place instantaneously, and at about between half-past ten and eleven o'clock. And the murdered man had been robbed—there was no money on him. Who was the murderer—and thief? About ten o'clock that night—that is to say, a quarter of an hour before Roger Maidment left Hagsdene Park—two credible and respectable witnesses, Ellen Hopkinson and James Collier, saw Richard Radford enter Hagsdene Wood. They saw him conceal his bicycle between the hedge and some bushes: after taking from it a parcel and a stout stick, he went into the wood by a path which would take him close by the spot where Maidment's dead body was subsequently found. Nothing was known of Richard Radford's movements or whereabouts during that night: from the time of his being seen by James Collier and Ellen Hopkinson all trace of him was lost, and he himself, questioned, absolutely refused to give any account of his doings. But at half-past ten next morning he called on one Fardale, a bookmaker, and paid him fifty-one pounds, a betting debt which he had owed for some time, and for which Fardale had been pressing him. He handed Fardale forty-five pounds in banknotes and six pounds in gold—the gold in sovereigns. And among these sovereigns was the perforated sovereign which Collingwood had paid to Roger Maidment the night before. Where had Richard Radford got it? On that point he was also obstinately silent, utterly refusing to say.

This was, practically, the full case for the prosecution: nevertheless, the setting of it out, and the hearing of witnesses in support, occupied the whole of a day. We jurymen—in charge, of course—were put up at a quiet hotel near the Assize Court, out of reach of the world, for this night. Next morning we heard the defence, which had been entrusted to a famous criminal barrister, Henshawe, Q.C. Henshawe was a bully—he bullied all the witnesses for the prosecution, and especially Fardale. But he did not succeed in shaking Fardale's evidence about the perforated sovereign. What Henshawe seemed to rely on for his defence was this—put together in a series of what appeared to be suggestions: (1) that the parcel spoken of by the witnesses Hopkinson and Collier contained books, three new novels, and that Richard Radford, when they saw him, was on his way to give them to somebody, presumably a lady, and that in the house of that somebody he spent the night, and had already arrived there at the time the murder was committed; (2) that the stick found in the wood and believed to have been the weapon with which the crime was committed was not the stick taken from his machine in Collier's and Hopkinson's presence; (3) that the banknotes handed by Richard Radford to Fardale were not identical with the banknotes paid by Hagsdene Park tenants to Roger Maidment; and (4) that it was impossible to prove that the perforated sovereign handed to Fardale by Richard Radford was the sovereign given to Maidment by Collingwood, pierced sovereigns being not at all uncommon in consequence of many men wearing them as pendants to watch-chains. Henshawe brought various evidence in support of all this—to my mind the most important witness was the accused lad's sister, Miss Audrey Radford.

After hearing both prosecution and defence and finding that the prisoner was determined to preserve the silence which had characterized him from the very beginning, I felt convinced that the case rested on the perforated sovereign, and I waited in some anxiety to hear what his lordship would say about it in his summing-up. We of the jury were, of course, all anxious to hear the summing-up—jurymen always are. But we did not get it until after the luncheon interval on the second day, and when it came it was very brief. My impression of it was that it was very much against the prisoner, and I had an uneasy feeling that his lordship felt that the youngster before him was defying Law and Everything by his determination to hold his tongue and must therefore take the consequences. And so, at three o'clock in the afternoon of the second day, we twelve good men and true were handed over to the charge of a stern-faced guardian whose duty it was to see that we were kept without meat, drink, or fire until we had decided whether Richard Radford should go free or whether he should be hanged by the neck till he was dead.

3

I now found myself in charge of the next proceedings. Here I was with eleven other men, none of them at all well known to me, though I certainly had a nodding acquaintance with each of them, as we were all dwellers in the same district. But, as I shall be obliged to refer by name to those taking part in our discussions, I had better give the names of the twelve men in whose hands lay the fate of the lad now awaiting our verdict. The panel had been prepared from the lists of eligible persons in Grandminster and places adjacent, and when we had been finally marshalled, gone unchallenged (the prisoner did not exercise his right of challenge in any one instance), and been duly sworn, I found that each of four separate places, towns, or villages had contributed three members of this particular jury. But I had better be specific:

Septimus Nettleton, 51 Abbot's Way, Grandminster, Merchant. *Foreman.*
Henry Chettle, 3 Sampson Street, Grandminster, Auctioneer.
John Ashworth, 5 Ditmas Street, Grandminster, Draper.
Charles Maydue, Home Farm, Petherton Magna, Farmer.
Arthur Jennings, Woodman Inn, Petherton Magna, Publican.
William Ewbank, North Lodge, Petherton Magna, Estate Agent.
William Coward, 8 High Street, Hebsworth, Accountant.
John Heaviside, 16 High Street, Hebsworth, Grocer.
Thomas Milford, 4 Beech Grove, Hebsworth, Clerk.
Charles Williams, 6 Market Place, Riverley, Saddler.
Thomas Crabtree, Red Lion Hotel, Riverley, Licensed Victualler.
William Sergeant, Chequers Place, Riverley, Farmer.

It will be seen from this list what sort of men we were in whose hands this tremendous issue lay—just twelve very ordinary Englishmen—every one of us engaged in business of one sort or another, none of us connected in any way with the Law. And I think the first feeling we had, when we had been duly locked up in a big, somewhat ornately furnished room (it was, as a matter of fact, the Lord Mayor of Grandminster's parlour, and its walls were heavy with obese gentlemen in furred gowns and gold chains), in which a bright fire burned and there were comfortable elbow chairs set round a great oval table, was one of relief that we had escaped from the sombre and sordid atmosphere of the Assize Court.

'They don't seem to keep to the strict letter of the Law, I think, Mr Foreman,' remarked Mr Maydue of Petherton Magna, as we gathered about the table. 'It said we were to be kept without meat, drink, or fire till we'd come to a decision, and there's a fire big enough to roast an ox—and very welcome, too, I'm sure—it's a cold and draughty place, that court.'

'Yes, and I dare say we could find a point stretched about meat and drink if need be,' observed Mr Crabtree of Riverley. 'I've been on these jobs when that point was stretched, anyway. How long do you think we shall be talking, Mr Foreman?'

'That depends on how much talking is done, Mr Crabtree,' I replied. 'There must, of course, be an interchange of views.'

Mr Heaviside, the grocer of Hebsworth, who had attracted my attention during the trial by his evident restlessness and a series of impatient snorts, spoke—irritably.

'See no reason for any talking, Mr Foreman!' he rapped out. 'Clear as crystal, this here case is! Guilty—that's what I say.'

A murmur of deprecation ran round the table.

'Here, here!' said Mr Maydue. 'You're in a bit of a hurry, Mr Heaviside! Why, we haven't even started to consider things yet!'

'Take a deal of considering, in my opinion,' muttered Mr Jennings of Petherton Magna. 'Queer a case, this is, as ever I sat on. And I've sat on a few, gentlemen—'Sizes, and coroners! Very queer case!'

'Needs some talking about, I think,' opined Mr Williams of Riverley. 'Not one o' them cases that you can settle in a minute. Requires discussing.'

That gave me a handle. From my chair at the head of the big oval table I glanced round the ellipse of perplexed and wondering faces—all of them typical of rusticity.

'Gentlemen,' I said, 'let us begin by each one of us giving his own opinion of the case as it presents itself to him after hearing the evidence and his lordship's summing-up. When we have each spoken we shall have a general idea of where we are. If there is a general unanimity we shall soon arrive at a verdict. If there are differences of opinion we can discuss them. And, gentlemen, remember this—there is a man's life at stake! And he is a young man. Now let us each say his say.'

'Hear, hear!' said Mr Maydue. 'That's fair doings! You begin, then, Mr Foreman. Let's have your views.'

'With all respect to your suggestion, Mr Maydue,' I replied, 'I think it will be more in accordance with precedent if I speak last. As your foreman, you see, I am in something of the same position as his lordship in the court downstairs. I suggest that I should hear each of you gentlemen first, and then give my own opinion in summing up yours. Now, to be practical, let us begin at my right hand and go round the table. Mr Chettle!'

Mr Chettle, a well-known auctioneer of Grandminster, who was loud-voiced and eloquent enough when he was selling sheep, pigs, and cattle at the weekly auction mart, showed signs of perturbation and nervousness at being thus called on. He cleared his throat, pulled down his waistcoat, shook his head, and glanced questioningly from one to another of us.

'Well, I really don't know what to say, Mr Foreman,' he began. 'As Mr Jennings there said just now, this is a very queer case—never heard a queerer in my time! Of course, there's no doubt that this young man, Maidment, was murdered by somebody, and as far as I can see it was for what he had on him. Well, now, there's no doubt, either, that young Radford was hard up for money. We've heard that Fardale was pressing him for money, and had threatened him with what he'd do if he didn't get his money by a certain time. Well, Fardale did get his money! Now where did young Radford get that money? We've heard that he was in or about Hagsdene Wood that night—I see no reason to doubt the evidence of the young woman, Ellen Hopkinson, and her young man, on that point. And it seems certain that Maidment had some hundred pounds or so—a hundred pounds, wasn't it?—on him, some of it in banknotes and six pounds in gold. It's certain, too, there was none of that money on him when his dead body was found. Well, now, Collingwood swears that when he paid his rent to Maidment he gave him a sovereign through which somebody had drilled a hole. Fardale swears that young Radford gave him that sovereign next morning—that very sovereign, according to him and Collingwood. Where did young Radford get it? The prosecution says he took it from Maidment's pocket. Well, of course, if that is so, there's only one conclusion to come to. But I'm not certain! As you said, Mr Foreman, there's a man's life at stake, and a young man's at that, and I want to be careful. There's certain things that I'm not satisfied about. I'm not satisfied about that sovereign. Then there's the question of the sticks. Those two witnesses I mentioned said young Radford had a stick on his machine and they saw him take it off and carry it away into the wood with him, but they couldn't swear that it was the stick the policeman found in the rabbit-burrow. Now that was an oak stick—common as blackberries. But the sister, Miss Audrey, swore that that—the oak stick—was not the stick her brother took out of the house with him when he left that evening—what he fastened on his bicycle, in her presence, was an ash-plant stick. I believe her!—and I see no reason why young Radford should have exchanged his ash-plant for an oak stick. Then there's the question of the banknotes paid by young Radford to Fardale. According to the evidence we got—you'll correct me if I'm wrong, Mr Foreman—those were not the banknotes, nor any of 'em, paid by Hagsdene Park tenants to Maidment. True, the prosecution suggested that they needn't have been—that Maidment may have had, and probably had, other money, more banknotes on him. But they brought no evidence to show that he had! If they could have shown that Maidment had collected rents late that afternoon, after the banks had closed, and had the money on him when he went to Hagsdene Park, there might have been something in it, but they didn't show that. I'm by no means assured that the notes and gold which young Radford handed to Fardale came from Maidment's pockets, and if it didn't I see no case against him. What I do feel about the whole thing is that there's a very deep and queer mystery somewhere behind this affair, and that we haven't heard anything to solve it—and, in my opinion, aren't likely to! That's all I've got to say, Mr Foreman.'

There was a murmur of what I took to be approval of Mr Chettle's views when he had spoken his last word, and I began to see how things were likely to go. I turned to Mr Chettle's next neighbour.

'Mr Ashworth!'

Mr Ashworth was a man whom I knew very well—a draper in Grandminster. He was a quiet, unassuming little man, but there was an air of confidence about him when he spoke, and he was emphatically the sort of man whose word was at any time likely to carry weight in counsel.

'I don't think there's much doubt about the truth of those last remarks of Mr Chettle's, Mr Foreman,' he remarked, with a dry smile.

'It seems to me, after hearing all the evidence for and against, that I'm no nearer a solution of the problem than when I came here yesterday morning! Of course, I'm bearing in mind the fact that the prisoner has elected not to give evidence. I feel pretty certain why! Questions would have been put to him which he's no mind to answer—I don't say, though, that his answers would necessarily have incriminated himself. If I'm asked—or, as you ask me for my opinion, it's just this—I'm not satisfied with the evidence. There's no doubt that this young man had been pressed for money by Fardale, and no doubt, either, that he got the money with which to satisfy Fardale's demands. But I'm not convinced that he got it from Maidment. I think everything we've heard goes to prove that Richard Radford, pressed by Fardale under a threat, had a friend somewhere about to whom he could turn in an emergency. I think he turned to that friend, got the money from that friend, spent the night of October 17 with that friend. You may say, Mr Foreman—I see you are itching to pull me up!—you may say we've no evidence of that, but I think we had evidence—by inference, if nothing else. Radford hadn't the money on October 17; on October 18 he had, and by an early hour in the morning. But where did he spend the intervening night? I say we've a right, we jurymen, to draw a conclusion—he spent it with the person who lent or gave him the money: I think all the evidence points to that. Frankly, on the evidence put before us, I don't believe that any of the money, either banknotes or gold, which Radford handed over to Fardale came from Maidment. The perforated sovereign incident I simply ignore!—there isn't one of us here that hasn't seen a score of sovereigns at one time or another with holes drilled in them! As to Radford's being in or near, or passing through, Hagsdene Wood at about the same time that Maidment was approaching it, I set that down to a mere coincidence. Taking it altogether, Mr Foreman, I see no grounds for a conviction in this case—though I'm bound to say that the police couldn't do otherwise than prosecute. Anyway, the evidence we've heard is not, in my opinion, strong enough to justify us in finding a verdict of guilty. That's my view of things!'

Again there was a murmur of approval—I began to think that we should not be kept there very long.

'Mr Maydue!' I said. 'Your opinion.'

Mr Maydue, a jollyfaced farmer, leaned over the table, rubbing his big hands and obviously glad of the opportunity of airing his sentiments.

'Well, I'll tell you what my opinion is, Mr Foreman, in a very few words,' he said. 'My opinion, sir, is just this here—I believe that if yon lad in the dock didn't do it—and I don't say that he did, for, mind you, I'm more than doubtful on that point—but if he didn't, well, sir, and gentlemen all, he knows who did! And it's my opinion too, Mr Foreman, that he got that sovereign from the fellow who did—whoever he may be! What that young fellow's doing, gentlemen, is this here—he's shielding the real murderer. And why?—that's what I want to know. Whatever any of the rest of you may think I believe that the sovereign with the hole in it, which young Radford gave to Fardale, is the sovereign that Collingwood gave to Maidment. I don't see no way, sir, of getting round the evidence of Collingwood and Fardale on that point. And I say again, I think young Radford could say who did kill Maidment. That's what I've got to say, sir!—short and sweet!'

Mr Maydue leaned back in his chair, satisfied and determined. I had to bring him to the point.

'I'm afraid we're not called on for opinions of that sort, Mr Maydue,' I said gently. 'What we've got to decide is—did Richard Radford kill Roger Maidment?—yes or no? That's all we're concerned with. Now, what's your opinion on that issue?'

Mr Maydue shook his head.

'Oh—ah—well!' he said. 'If I'm to give a plain answer to that, Mr Foreman, all I can say is—no, I don't believe he did!'

I looked at Mr Maydue's right-hand neighbour, Mr Jennings, the publican from Petherton Magna.

'What does Mr Jennings think?' I asked.

Mr Jennings was as slow to speak as Mr Maydue, his fellow-villager, had been ready.

'Well, Mr Foreman,' he replied hesitatingly, 'I think this is one of them cases in which there's a deal to be said on all sides. It's my opinion that them lawyer gentlemen has left a deal out that ought to ha' been put in. And I think this young man could tell a lot if he would. And I would like to know, sir, before we go any further, if there isn't any way of making the young fellow speak. Couldn't his lordship make him tell what he knows? For I'm sure he knows a good deal.'

'I'm afraid that's impossible, Mr Jennings,' I replied. 'Not all the judges on the bench can make a prisoner give evidence if he doesn't want to. We must leave that suggestion alone.'

'Aye, well, it's a pity, in my opinion,' continued Mr Jennings. 'I would like to hear what that young fellow has to say. As for the rest of it, I'm a good deal in agreement with my friend Mr Maydue. I think this lad's shielding somebody—the somebody who did it. And of course, if I think that, I don't think the lad did it himself. And—and—well, I don't know that I've any more to say, Mr Foreman, except that it's a very queer business altogether.'

'Mr Ewbank,' I said.

Mr Ewbank was well known in our neighbourhood as an estate agent managing several considerable properties, and as a businesslike, level-headed man, and I was very anxious to hear his views.

'It seems to me, Mr Foreman,' said Mr Ewbank, 'that there is no need for us to go outside the evidence put before us by the prosecution. We can't, indeed, go outside it if we would—our oath confines us to the evidence brought forward in court. Now in my opinion you can boil down the evidence against Richard Radford to this: Was the money, the actual notes and gold, which he admits giving to Fardale——'

'When did he admit that?' asked Mr Chettle. 'He hasn't given evidence!'

'That came out in Superintendent Henderson's evidence,' replied Mr Ewbank. 'Richard Radford stated, explicitly, more than once, that he did pay Fardale fifty-one pounds on the morning of October 18. Well, I say, was that money the actual notes and gold, so paid by him to Fardale, the same money, the same so much paper, so much coin, which Maidment received from the tenants at Hagsdene Park? If it was, then we want to know—the Law wants to know—how Richard Radford became possessed of it. Did he murder Maidment for it? Did he find Maidment murdered by somebody else, and, being hard up for money, possess himself of Maidment's money? He refuses to say—anything. Well, it goes back to my question—were the banknotes, were the sovereigns paid to Fardale, those paid to Maidment by the various tenants at Hagsdene Park? Let us leave the sovereigns aside for the moment and give our attention to the banknotes. Now what was the evidence about these?—I mean about the banknotes paid to Maidment? Gentlemen, the banknotes paid to Maidment by the Hagsdene Park tenants were, according to their sworn evidence, nearly all brand-new ones! But the notes handed to Fardale were all old, well-used ones. Therefore the notes paid to Fardale by Richard Radford were certainly not the notes paid to Maidment at Hagsdene Park. That is certain!'

Mr Ewbank paused for a moment to look round the table. Most of us nodded our approval. But Mr Heaviside made a grunt of dissent.

'Well,' continued Mr Ewbank, 'I think that disposes of the notes. But there has been a suggestion made that Maidment may have been carrying money other than that which he collected at Hagsdene Park;

that he may have had two or three hundred pounds on him. But the prosecution brought forward no evidence whatever to that effect! If Maidment had been collecting rents or payments elsewhere than Hagsdene Park on October 17 and had, in consequence, a lot of money in his pockets, why didn't the prosecution bring evidence to prove that? The prosecution brought no evidence. So we can throw that suggestion aside. Then we come to the marked sovereign—or, rather, the perforated sovereign. Well, with all respect to both of them, I must say that I was surprised that either Mr Collingwood or Mr Fardale would positively swear on that point! We every one of us know that it—as the defence suggested—is no uncommon thing for men to wear a sovereign as a pendant to a watch-chain, and how any man can swear that *a* sovereign is *the* sovereign seems to me as foolish as swearing that *a* pea is *the* pea. And——'

'But you'll excuse me, Mr Ewbank,' interrupted Mr Heaviside from his end of the table. 'Fardale swore that when he received that sovereign from Radford junior, he put it in a certain pocket and never touched it again until Collingwood told him of the murder. How do you get over that, now?'

'I get over it,' replied Mr Ewbank coolly, 'by saying, first, that Mr Fardale is as liable to make a mistake in matters of memory as any other man, and, second, that if Richard Radford did give Fardale a perforated sovereign it was no proof that it was the identical sovereign with a hole drilled in it which was given by Collingwood to Maidment. There is such a thing as coincidence in this world, gentlemen, and just to show you that there is, I myself have one sovereign in my pocket which has a hole in it, and I have another—here!'

With these words Mr Ewbank snapped off his watch-chain and threw it on the table before him; after which he produced another sovereign from his pocket. A murmur went round the table and somebody became vocal.

'There are lots of 'em about—my father always carried one on his chain. Said it would come in handy if he was ever broke!'

'Well, gentlemen,' continued Mr Ewbank, resuming possession of his exhibits, 'I think it would be a very foolish thing to find a man, and a young man, guilty of murder on evidence of that sort. But there is another matter—that of the stick; it has been referred to before, but I want to refer to it myself. The prosecution produced an oak stick—the sort of common oak walking-stick that you can buy anywhere for a shilling—which was discovered hidden away in Hagsdene Wood, and they suggest that it was with that stick that Maidment was done to death and that it—that particular stick—was one which had been given by Hebb, Mr Radford senior's clerk, to young Richard Radford: Hebb identified it as such. Now I don't believe that Hebb could identify that stick! You could buy sticks like that, as the witness Shillaker said, by the score. But there's something more than that. Young Radford undoubtedly had a stick with him when he entered Hagsdene Wood: I see no reason to doubt the evidence of James Collier and Ellen Hopkinson on that point. But what stick? Now we have evidence that what he fastened on his bicycle when he left his father's house was an ash-plant stick. That evidence was given by his sister, Miss Audrey Radford. Hers was straightforward evidence. An ash-plant stick!—well, where is it? I think I know. Richard Radford left that ash-plant in the house where he stopped the night—in the house of the person he's shielding!'

'Ah—then you agree he is shielding somebody, Mr Ewbank?' exclaimed Mr Jennings. 'You think that, sir—just as I do?'

'I certainly think that,' replied Mr Ewbank. 'I——'

'Shielding the actual murderer?' persisted Mr Jennings.

'No!' said Mr Ewbank. 'He's shielding some woman! Mr Foreman, my opinion, my considered opinion, after hearing all the evidence, is that young Radford knows nothing whatever about the actual murder, did not get the banknotes nor the sovereign from Maidment, dead or alive, and that his presence near the scene of the crime is mere coincidence. I am for a verdict of not guilty!'

This was direct enough, and once more I felt that we should not be long in arriving at a decision. But there was still other members of the jury left to speak, and I called on the next.

'Mr Coward!'

Mr Coward turned an inquiring eye on me.

'I don't know if I should be in order in referring to a little matter which didn't exactly come in evidence before us, Mr Foreman?' he said. 'But there is something—perhaps there's one or two things—that I could mention that might throw a bit of light, though, of course, I don't want to do or say anything irregular.'

'All friends here!' said somebody. 'Confidential!'

'What is it, Mr Coward?' I replied. 'If it relates to the case—and, even indirectly, to the evidence——'

'Well, it's just this, Mr Foreman,' continued Mr Coward. 'You see, there's been a suggestion that Maidment might have had money on him other than that he got from those people at Hagsdene Park. Well, now, I knew Maidment very well indeed—being an accountant myself, I had business dealings with him, and, as a matter of fact, before Maidment set up for himself at Ullathwaite he was in my employ as a clerk for a time. Now I'm quite sure, from what I know of him and his habits, that when he set out to Hagsdene Park that night, to collect the rents there, he wouldn't carry money with him. If he'd collected any money that day, or had had money paid in to him at his office, it wouldn't be in his pockets! He was a careful chap about money. And the prosecution, mind you, didn't bring forward a single scrap of evidence to show that he had other money on him—it was nothing but a suggestion, unsupported by any evidence. I think we may take it as certain that all that Maidment had about him, when he was murdered, was the hundred and ten pounds in cheques, notes, and gold, which he'd just collected at Hagsdene Park. Well, now, there's no doubt whatever, as far as I can see, that the banknotes which this young Radford handed over to Mr Fardale, the bookmaker, were certainly not the banknotes collected from various tenants by Maidment. So I think there's clear proof that that bit of evidence has nothing in it, and that Radford did not get his money from that source. Is that relative to what we heard downstairs, Mr Foreman?'

'I think it is,' I replied. 'Decidedly so, Mr Coward.'

'Well, I don't suppose what I'm going to say now is, though,' responded Mr Coward. 'But I'll say it, for all that. Perhaps I ought to have told the police of something I know, but then I imagined they'd find it out for themselves. It's this—I happen to know, for a fact, that Maidment carried a revolver, all ready loaded. He bought it when he was with me, because he used to collect rents at night in those days, out in the country, and he wanted something to protect himself with. And I say this, Mr Foreman, because I think it shows that Maidment was laid in wait for and struck down suddenly in Hagsdene Wood——'

'I'm afraid we've no evidence of that before us, Mr Coward,' I interrupted. 'All we know is that he was struck down. And our duty is to say by whose hand, or, rather, if it was by the hand of the prisoner in our charge.'

'Very well, sir,' said Mr Coward, 'then I'll say that I can't persuade myself that it was! The dissimilarity in the notes is enough for me, and I pay no attention to the marked coin.'

Mr Coward sat down, and I looked at his right-hand neighbour, Mr Heaviside. Mr Heaviside, it will be remembered, was the man who, as soon as we had assembled ourselves round the table, had gruffly remarked that he saw no reason for any talking, that the case was clear as crystal, and that he considered Richard Radford guilty. And while the successive opinions were being given I had been watching Mr Heaviside, for I foresaw trouble with him. He was the sort of man, in my view, who would make trouble anywhere—surly, stupid, bad-tempered. While his fellow-jurymen had said their say, he had kept up a ceaseless comment of grunts, groans, and sighs, indicative of his intense disapproval. And now, when his turn came, he lost no time in showing us the state of his feelings.

'It's a fair marvel to me that all this talk should go on, Mr Foreman!' he exclaimed irritably. 'I've sat on a many juries in my time, and heard some queer evidence for and against, but I've never heard no clearer than I heard yesterday and this morning in yon court! There can't but be one verdict in this case, and that verdict's—guilty! I've been naught less than amazed to hear what's been said by some of you gentlemen sitting round this table—I should ha' thought you'd ha' made up your minds in five minutes. Yon there young rapscallion murdered and robbed Maidment, and that's the long and short of it. God bless my soul!—to hear the opinions that's just been expressed, Mr Foreman, you'd think that them as expressed 'em had no idea of the value of evidence. Now you can't put me down!' added Mr Heaviside as ominous murmurs of dissent and disapprobation arose round the table. 'I've as much right to my opinion as what you have, and I shan't be silenced by nobody. As I said to start with, it's a fair marvel to me that there should be aught but one opinion in this case. Was Maidment murdered? Is there any doubt of it? Was Maidment robbed of his money? There's no doubt about that, neither! Was this here young Radford—a bad lot at all times!—hanging around yon Hagsdene Wood at what we'll call the critical moment? We know that he was. Was he hard up for money? It's admitted. Did he pay Fardale fifty-one pounds next morning? We know he did. Where did he get it?—he'd not got it the day before—where did he get it between then and next morning? Did he give Fardale a certain marked coin that Mr Collingwood of Hagsdene Park had paid to Maidment? I believe that he did—and I say he's guilty! I've been on a many juries, Mr Foreman, but I never knew such what I may term inability to face facts as I've seen to-day—I should ha' thought that every one of you when you came out o' that jury-box to this room—a proceeding that I consider sheer waste of time, and absolutely unnecessary—would ha' been agreed upon a verdict, and that verdict what I say—guilty! Anyway, I know the value of evidence when I hear it, and I say guilty, and I shall go on saying it if I sit here till Doomsday! Guilty o' murder—that's my verdict!'

Mr Heaviside ceased his exordium among further deprecating murmurs. I turned to the man on his right hand.

'Mr Milford!'

Mr Milford, a clerk in a wholesale warehouse, was a nervous, timid little person, obviously without any relish for the duties thrust upon him. He edged away from his neighbour, as if afraid of him.

'I—I—I'm afraid I can't agree with Mr Heaviside, Mr Foreman,' he began. 'I—the fact is, sir, I can't get over the evidence about the banknotes, sir, and I don't feel satisfied about the sovereign with a hole in it. I don't think the evidence is conclusive, sir——'

'More fool you!' snapped out Mr Heaviside. 'Clear as daylight!'

'Mr Heaviside!' I said, as sternly as possible. 'I must call you to order. You must not interrupt these proceedings, nor comment on the opinions of others while they are being given. Yes, Mr Milford?'

'Well, sir,' resumed Mr Milford, 'I—I've only got to say that I agree with most of the gentlemen who have spoken. I—shouldn't feel justified in saying the young man was guilty, sir—on the evidence.'

'Thank you, Mr Milford,' I said. 'Now—Mr Williams.'

Mr Williams was a bluff, cheery-faced man, a saddler by trade; he had a hearty open-air look about him, and he gave us all a sort of well-now-come-let's-be-a-bit-merciful smile as he responded to my invitation.

'Well, Mr Foreman!' he said, as if he were pleading for indulgence for some erring child. 'What bit I've got to say is just this, and as we're all more or less of sportsmen, I reckon you'll understand my meaning. It seems to me we're in the position of umpires at cricket: it's for us to say "out" or "not out"! Now, as you all very well know, whenever there's a doubt about a decision at cricket, the batsman's entitled to the benefit of it. That's fair—that's sport, 'cause he's one against eleven. Now, in my opinion, there's a considerable doubt in this case, and, that being so, I think the young fellow downstairs ought to have the benefit of it. I'm for letting him off—I don't agree with Mr Heaviside at all. I say not guilty!'

'Who cares whether you agree with me or no?' growled Mr Heaviside. 'I would like to know which is the best judge—me or you? I've been——'

'Order, order!' I said sternly. 'We have still two more opinions to listen to. Mr Crabtree—what do you say?'

Mr Crabtree was even shyer and more nervous than Mr Milford. He was a heavy, sleepy sort of man, who up to then had sat, open-mouthed, twiddling his two big thumbs and staring anxiously at each successive speaker. On my addressing him, he started, and shook his head.

'Well, Mr Foreman, sir,' he said diffidently, 'I'm no great scholar, and I would ha' liked to be out o' this job—it's not in my line at all. But I listened careful downstairs, and I've listened careful here, sir, and I'm inclined to side with Mr Williams there. It seems to me, sir, that there's a deal o' doubt about this case, and I think the young man ought to have the benefit. I wouldn't like to say that I consider him guilty, myself. That's all that I can think of to say, Mr Foreman—as I say, I'm no scholar, and no lawyer, but, wanting to be fair and right, such is my opinion, sir.'

'Very much obliged to you, Mr Crabtree,' I said. 'Now let us hear Mr Sergeant's opinion.'

Mr Sergeant, another rustic gentleman, was possessed of a similar spirit of diffidence. He too shook his head doubtfully as he opened his lips.

'Why, sir,' he began, 'there seems to be some dispute between us on this here matter. Most of the gentlemen that's spoken says one thing, and Mr Heaviside says another. I think, myself, it's a very doubtful matter. And I've been wondering, Mr Foreman—I've never been on a jury before, so you'll excuse me if I say aught that's wrong—but I've been wondering if I couldn't make a proposal?'

'Certainly, Mr Sergeant,' I replied. 'What is it?'

'Well, couldn't we send downstairs to his lordship and ask him to tell us what to say? I'm very sure, sir,' continued Mr Sergeant, looking his wonder at the smiles which his suggestion produced, 'I'm very sure that his lordship knows a great deal more about it than we do, and whatever he said, I should be agreeable to. If——'

'I'm afraid that's quite out of the question, Mr Sergeant,' I said. 'We are the sole arbiters of this young man's fate! It is for us to say whether he's guilty or not guilty. Nobody can question our verdict. Nobody can ask us to give any reason for our verdict. And our verdict is final. Have you any more to say, Mr Sergeant?'

'Nay, I think not, sir,' replied Mr Sergeant, 'except, in the main, I agree with Mr Crabtree and Mr Williams. Wherever there's a doubt, I think the young fellow downstairs ought to benefit. Hanging's a very serious matter, sir.'

'Give us your views, Mr Foreman,' said one or two members, speaking together. 'Sum things up, like. And then let's know where we are,' added another. 'It'll be an anxious time for yon lad, waiting to know what's going to be done with him!'

I need not set down what I said in answer to this request. I had formed my own opinion about the evidence before ever we retired from the jury-box. I did not think that evidence strong enough to justify a conviction, and I said so now, and gave my reasons. And that done, I suggested that I should now take a show of hands, so that we might know definitely where, after more than three and a half hours' talk, we had got to.

This I immediately did. The result was as follows:

For an acquittal—eleven.
For a conviction—one.

The one, of course, was Mr Heaviside. And, looking at his grim and determined countenance, I realized that he was going to give still more trouble.

4

An awkward silence followed Mr Heaviside's emphatic declaration, and, of course, it fell to my lot to break it.

'Mr Heaviside,' I said, as politely as possible, 'there are eleven of us in favour of an acquittal: you are the only one against it. May I suggest that you should reconsider matters?'

'You can suggest what you please, sir!' he replied sourly. 'I've said my say, and it's all I intend to say. I've as much right to my opinion as what any other gentleman has——'

'We're not questioning your rights at all, Mr Heaviside,' I said. 'All I'm asking you to do is to—think again! Here we are, twelve of us—eleven of us are unanimous——'

He let out a scornful exclamation.

'Unanimous!' he sneered. 'Why, there's them here'—he pointed to two or three of the last speakers—'two or three here as hasn't got minds o' their own! They'd say anything if need be! Them at this end o' the table has only voted with you for the sake of agreement. I'm made o' different stuff, I am! I say guilty—and I mean it and shall say no other. It makes no difference to me if the voting's eleven to one—one's as good as eleven in a case o' this sort. Didn't I take the oath same as all of you? What's that oath say? "According to the evidence." What? Well, I've listened to the evidence, and I say—guilty!'

Amidst a murmur of dissenting voices Mr Maydue spoke.

'Mr Foreman,' he said, 'doesn't it go by a majority? If there's seven for, and five against, for instance, doesn't the seven have it?'

'No!' I replied. 'The verdict must be unanimous.'

'Wouldn't it do,' persisted Mr Maydue, 'if we went back and said that eleven of us were for not guilty, and one for guilty?'

'No!' I said. 'It would not do at all. Whatever verdict is given, it must be the verdict of all of us.'

'And supposing,' asked Mr Williams, 'supposing, sir, that he'—here he cocked a thumb at Mr Heaviside—'supposing he won't come to our way of thinking, what should we do?'

'We go back to court, Mr Williams, and report that we are unable to agree upon a verdict,' I replied.

'That's a nice state of affairs!' remarked Mr Crabtree. 'We shall look a nice lot, not to be able to say one way or another!'

'I hope we shall come to an agreement yet, gentlemen,' I said. 'I think that Mr Heaviside, if he reflects a little, will see that it will be in the interests of justice if he falls in with our view of the case. Just think the matter over again, Mr Heaviside! And, as you're probably aware, if there's any point on which you wish for further light, it's always possible to approach his lordship for counsel, or explanation——'

'I want no counsel nor yet explanation from his lordship, nor from you neither!' retorted Mr Heaviside angrily. 'What I want is to see you gentlemen come round to my way o' thinking. I want a conviction! It's a fair puzzle to me that you can think otherwise than what I do. Yon lad there—a real young bad 'un!—murdered and robbed Maidment as sure as my name's what it is, and a name, mind you, that's held in high respect, and I consider that it 'ud be nothing less than a disgrace to let a young scamp like that go free on the world and society again. And I've been on many a jury before, and I know what lasting it out means, and I'm prepared for it. I've seen a case or two like this in my time, and I've known where a minority of two or three has beaten a majority of eight or nine, and I reckon I've as much endurance as what you have! I'm prepared to sit here all the rest of the afternoon, and all the evening, and all the night, if need be—I came prepared!'

With these words, and with a scornful smile of superiority, Mr Heaviside produced from one pocket a very capacious flask, and from another a large packet of what appeared to be sandwiches, and waved both triumphantly in our faces.

Out of a general murmur of disapproval and resentment which ran all round the table Mr Maydue's voice made itself heard.

'I should say more than one can play at that game, Mr Foreman,' he said. 'Mr Heaviside mustn't think that he's going to get the better of us in that way! I've got an old encyclopædia at home, and I read up in it about the duties and privileges and so on of jurymen before I came here to these Assizes. Now it certainly says that juries are to be kept "without meat, drink, or fire" until they arrive at a verdict, but it also says that they can have reasonable refreshment if ordered by the Judge. And as Mr Heaviside seems inclined to dare us, Mr Foreman, I move that you take steps to get the rest of us some tea. It's getting on to seven o'clock.'

Amidst a murmur of gratification at Mr Maydue's suggestion—countered by a sort of obvious defiance from Mr Heaviside—I approached our guardian patiently waiting outside our door, and intimated that, subject to his lordship's approval, we should like some refreshment. He looked at me narrowly.

'Likely to be long, sir?' he inquired.

'Some little time,' I replied, guardedly. 'We are not yet in view of a unanimous agreement—it is a difficult case.'

'It's like this, you see, sir,' he said, confidentially, 'if it's going to be say another hour or so, I should say—well, a cup of tea and a mouthful of bread and butter. But if you're likely to be rather long over it—well, then, I should suggest tea and something more substantial—sandwiches, eh?'

'I think you had better say sandwiches,' I answered. 'It is now some time since lunch, and there is still a good deal to talk about.'

He nodded intelligently, and I went back and was duly locked up with my eleven fellow-jurors again. Mr Ewbank approached me: I had already noticed that the ten men who were for an acquittal had risen from the table and were standing about the big room in groups, talking. Only Mr Heaviside remained at the table. He sat where I had left him, and he was busy with his flask and his sandwiches.

'I should like a word with you, Mr Foreman,' said Mr Ewbank. 'There's something I think you ought to know.'

'Yes?' I replied. 'What is it?'

He turned and motioned Mr Coward, the accountant from Hebsworth, to come to us. We moved away from the others into a quiet corner of the big room. Looking from one to the other I saw that both seemed to be impressed by whatever it was they wanted to say.

'Mr Foreman,' began Ewbank, 'Mr Coward here has been telling me something, and I consider what he's told me to be of a very serious nature and that you should be made aware of it before we go any further. The fact is, Mr Foreman, that after hearing what Mr Coward has just told me I'm of the decided opinion that Mr Heaviside's attitude is not due to his conception of this case—I mean his conception of the evidence—but to a personal prejudice. He never ought to have been on this jury!'

'What do you mean by personal prejudices?' I asked. 'Do you mean against the prisoner?'

'No, sir, but against the prisoner's father and mother!' replied Ewbank. 'According to Mr Coward, Mr Heaviside has cherished a personal prejudice against Mr and Mrs Radford for some three-and-twenty years! Indeed, it's more than a prejudice—it's a desire for revenge. He's been heard to say——'

'Not of late, you know,' interrupted Coward. 'Years ago, it was.'

'Well, that makes little difference,' said Ewbank. 'He's been heard to say that he'd bide his time but he'd have his revenge on them both! And—here's his chance, if he could persuade the rest of us.'

'But why does he wish to be revenged on Mr and Mrs Radford?' I asked. 'What is it all about?'

Ewbank jerked a thumb at Coward.

'Mr Coward here can tell you,' he said. 'He's a fellow-townsman of Heaviside's, and he's known him all his life.'

'It's like this, Mr Foreman,' said Coward as I turned to him. 'I shouldn't have mentioned it if I didn't feel convinced that Heaviside's attitude is just due to a long-cherished desire to get his knife into the Radford family. I don't believe he thinks that this lad, young Richard, killed Maidment, nor that he'd care twopence if he did! All he wants is to strike a blow at the lad's father and mother.'

'But why?' I asked.

'For this reason,' he answered, drawing me a little farther aside. 'You see, as Mr Ewbank there says, Heaviside is a fellow-townsman, and, in fact, close neighbour—his shop is only a few doors from my office. I've known Heaviside all my life—we were boys together at school. Now, when Heaviside was a young man and had just got nicely established in his business, he fell madly in love with a young lady who had recently come to the town as second mistress at the Girls' High School. Well, now, Heaviside was on the committee of management of the school, and no sooner had the young lady come than he fell madly in love with her, and wasn't at all slow to let her know of it! He wasn't the surly, black-tempered man that he is now, but he was even then a very masterful, domineering sort of fellow, and he was bent on getting his own way in everything——'

'He's not altered much in that respect!' I remarked.

'Got worse, sir,' agreed Coward. 'Well, I don't know how much headway he made with the young lady, but anyway I do remember that when she'd been in Hebsworth some few months and Heaviside was keener on her than ever, the old gentleman who'd been clerk to the committee of the Girls' High School died, and Mr Radford, of Ullathwaite, was appointed in his place. Now Mr Radford was a very good-looking young fellow, well-to-do, and a rising man, and, of course, a professional man and well educated, whereas Heaviside was uneducated and a tradesman. And Radford fell in love with the young lady, and no doubt he appealed to her a good deal more than Heaviside did, and to make a long story short, Radford clean cut Heaviside out! As a matter of fact, there was a very short courtship and engagement, and Radford and the young lady were married.'

'And the young lady you refer to is the present Mrs Radford?' I inquired. 'Mother of the prisoner?'

'Exactly, sir—Mrs Radford, at present Mayoress of Ullathwaite,' replied Coward. 'Well, now, here's the point. Heaviside, of course, was not only a deeply disappointed man, but a furious one. He considered he'd been badly treated by the young lady—he said she'd encouraged him until Radford came on the scene. And he vowed he'd have his revenge on the two of them, however long he had to wait for it. And you know, Mr Foreman, he's never married!'

'Never married, eh?' I exclaimed. 'Ah!'

'He's never married,' repeated Coward. 'He's just gone on, making money, sour, dour, determined, brooding over things, but in my opinion always looking out for a chance to get even with those two. He's a revengeful man by nature. And now that he has got a chance——'

'He can do nothing,' I said, interrupting him. 'If he refuses to fall in with the rest of us, we shall simply report to his lordship that we're unable to agree, and there'll have to be a new trial.'

'Aye!' said Coward. 'But in my opinion, that's just what he's after! He thinks, I'm sure, that if there's a new trial this lad may be found guilty. And in any case he'll have given the father and mother the pain and anxiety of further suspense.'

'Is there nothing that could be done, Mr Foreman?' asked Ewbank. 'Couldn't this be reported to the Judge?'

'That would bring the thing to an end at once,' I said. 'Of course, Heaviside should have been challenged when the jury was being sworn. I wonder Mr Radford senior didn't think of it.'

'I suppose he didn't want to rake up old troubles,' replied Ewbank, 'or perhaps it never occurred to him that Heaviside was still revengeful. Anyway, there it is! And what's to be done?'

At that moment the welcome tea, accompanied by a generous supply of sandwiches, arrived, and, remarking to my two consultants that I'd think the matter over while we refreshed ourselves, I summoned the others to the side table on which the trays had been set out and proceeded to fortify them for further trials of their patience.

For I was determined to get at a verdict, and at the verdict of which eleven of us had already approved, if I could by any means do it. And while I sipped my tea and nibbled at a sandwich, I thought out my next method of procedure. As soon as my fellow-members had refreshed themselves I assembled them once more round the table, and, commanding attention, assumed a judicial tone.

'Now, gentlemen,' I said, 'as foreman of this jury I conceive it my duty to arrive at a verdict in this case. We know now how we stand. There are eleven of us for an acquittal. Unfortunately, there is one of us who is equally resolved on a conviction. That one is Mr Heaviside. Mr Heaviside is quite within his rights. But I think Mr Heaviside has failed to appreciate the fact that the weight of evidence is in the prisoner's favour. So, for Mr Heaviside's benefit, and with a view to affording him the opportunity of changing his mind——'

'Which I shan't do!' growled Mr Heaviside. 'Not on any account!'

'—I propose to review the whole case,' I continued, 'and I invite Mr Heaviside's strict attention to what I shall say——'

'Say what you like!' interrupted Mr Heaviside. 'Here I am, and here I stick! I reckon I can last you all out, if it comes to that.'

'I must remind you of your duty, Mr Heaviside,' I said. 'You are bound to listen to the opinions of your fellow-jurymen——'

'Heard 'em already!' he retorted. 'And reckon naught of 'em! But say your say, if you want to! All goes in at one ear and out at the other!'

I paid no further attention to his surly incivility, but proceeded to do exactly what I had said I would do. For two hours—during which the other members of the jury gave me their polite hearing, without sign of boredom or weariness—I treated Mr Heaviside to an elaborate recapitulation and analysis of the evidence, keeping my eyes fixed on him, and addressing myself entirely to him. And in spite of his sour and forbidding demeanour I saw that he listened. As soon as I had finished I asked for another vote. And once more Mr Heaviside was the sole dissentient to a verdict of acquittal.

It was now well past nine o'clock and time to take the step I had contemplated since hearing what Coward had to say. I rose from my chair, looking at Mr Heaviside, who at the moment was refreshing himself from his big flask.

'Mr Heaviside,' I said, 'may I have a word or two with you in private?'

He stared sullenly at me, but he left the table and joined me on the hearthrug. The room was a very-big one—big enough to separate us from the other ten.

'What do you want?' he demanded surlily. 'I've heard all you've got to say. And I've my right to my own opinion, same as you have.'

'Mr Heaviside,' I replied, 'I want to ask you to be a reasonable man. The weight of opinion is against you. Why not give in to it?'

'No!' he retorted. 'I've said so!'

'You persist in your attitude?' I asked.

'I stand by my rights!' he answered.

'Very well, Mr Heaviside,' I said. 'Then I may as well tell you what I am going to do. We are going to return to Court. I shall inform his lordship that I have made a most painful discovery, namely, that one of the jury, Mr John Heaviside, of Hebsworth, so far from being unbiased and unprejudiced, is actuated by a long-cherished feeling of malice and revenge against the prisoner's parents——'

He interrupted me with a growl or snarl of anger, and his eyes blazed as he turned from me to glare towards the table we had just left.

'That's yon damned Coward!' he exclaimed. 'He's been at you——'

'Isn't it true, Mr Heaviside?' I asked. 'Isn't it—hasn't it—been known in Hebsworth that you swore, years ago, to have your revenge on Radford and his wife? And now——'

'You daren't tell it out!' he growled. 'You wouldn't be let——'

'I shall tell every word to his lordship in open court!' I said. 'The circumstances are exceptional. You should never have been on this jury, Mr Heaviside—no honest man, had he felt what you do, would have accepted the duty. And when I've said what I shall say in court, where will you be, Mr Heaviside? You'll be disgraced for life! And I understand you're a man of some consequence in your town—and a churchwarden!'

He looked at me with something not unlike a threat in his small eyes, but he said nothing. I moved towards the table.

'So we'll go down—now!' I said.

'Stop!' he said, fetching his breath hard. 'What—what do you want me to do?'

'Fall in with the rest of us!' I said, promptly.

'And—it'll be shut mouths, thereafter?' he suggested.

'You may depend on that,' I answered.

He hesitated a moment; then he made a gesture as if he were baffled.

'Have it your own way!' he growled. 'My time'll come yet!'

Five minutes later, standing up in a crowded and breathlessly silent court, I heard a voice, swift, formal.

'Do you find the prisoner guilty or not guilty?'

Then I heard my own voice—as if a long way off.

'*Not Guilty!*'

And five minutes after that, stepping out of the jury-box, I found myself asking a question which I have been asking myself ever since: Who *did* kill Roger Maidment?

IV

THE TRUTH, THE WHOLE TRUTH...

(*Statement of Richard Radford*)

It is now some five-and-twenty years since I, at that time little more than a mere boy (I was, actually, just over legal age), stood in the dock of the Crown Court at Grandminster Assizes, awaiting—quite calmly, I remember, and with a curious confidence, born of I know not what conviction—the verdict of the twelve men on whose decision my life depended. That verdict, arrived at after hours of debate on their part and waiting on mine, was one of acquittal. Thirty-six hours previously I had been charged in set, formal terms, with the wilful murder of Roger Maidment. I had pleaded Not Guilty. The jury found me Not Guilty. There were people who believed me guilty before the trial and who continued to believe me guilty after the trial. There were people who believed me innocent, both before the trial and after it was over. Probably my guilt or innocence formed a staple subject of conversation in Ullathwaite for a long time. There were other people who could not make up their minds—and there were still others who were insatiably inquisitive. Among these was Mr P. W. Wrenne, who, as chairman of the local bench of magistrates, had presided over the initial proceedings of my prosecution. Mr Wrenne, with whom at a subsequent stage I became great friends, has often asked me, as its sole depository, to tell the truth about this case: he has felt all along, he says, that I always knew it. In that supposition he was not always correct: I did not always know it. I did not know it at the time of the trial; indeed, I did not know it for a good many years after the trial was over. But I guessed at it—and my guess eventually proved to be correct. But I never told anyone what my guess was: that I have kept to myself, jealously, until now. Now, at Mr Wrenne's suggestion, and, indeed, entreaty, I consent to tell the truth, the whole truth. . . .

I have had the opportunity—and taken it—of reading the statements, given to Mr Wrenne some five-and-twenty years ago, of those men who were concerned in this affair. And I have been struck by the fact that nobody, nobody at all, among all the people mentioned and referred to, ever had any suspicion of anybody but myself! I have often thought, of late, knowing what I do, that a very little reflection, a very little putting this-and-that together, would have fixed the killing of Roger Maidment on the man who did kill him. I am going to reveal the secret: why, this plain statement will reveal. But I could only have attempted the task, now or at any time, under certain conditions. They are now fulfilled by what people call the laws of nature: I mean, all the people whose names will have to come into this story are dead. My father and mother are dead. Henderson is dead: so is Wilsborough: so, I hear, is Nettleton, the foreman of the jury: so is Heaviside, who hated my parents and would gladly have seen me hanged to revenge himself on them. Mrs Norrington is dead: Mrs Hebb and her husband are dead: I, alone, am left of the *dramatis personæ*. No, there is one other left alive: my sister Audrey. But Audrey is dead to England: she married a man who carried her off to New Zealand, where he is now a big commercial magnate: I don't think Audrey will visit the old country again. And I am sure that she would approve my acquiescence in Mr Wrenne's suggestion. Truth, after all, is truth.

2

It was all owing to my having an occasional bet with Fardale, the bookmaker, that I became suspected of the murder of Roger Maidment. That—the betting business—had, of course, nothing whatever to do with the murder: Maidment, as I now know, would have been killed in any case; at least, killed under the circumstances which arose that evening. But if I had never betted with Fardale I should never have been in his power, nor in Hagsdene Wood on the night of the murder, nor in possession of the perforated sovereign about which such a fuss was made, and so——

But all that is useless for my present purpose: I did bet with Fardale, now and then, and on October 16, 1899, I owed him fifty-one pounds. If only a certain horse had come in first in a certain race a few days before, I shouldn't have owed Fardale anything at all, but instead of coming in first, or even second or third, it finished somewhere down the course, and accordingly—— But we need not go into that: I was never very lucky. Of course, I should never have betted at all, in my position, which was that of articled clerk to my own father. I think I found some relief, some necessary excitement, in it: things were dull at home. My mother, though the best of women, was severely Puritanical, and my sister and I knew from infancy what it was to be suppressed. I got some relief in cricket and football, but I wanted more than that, and betting on racehorses gave one at least an occasional thrill. It was at first a mere half-crown business; then five shillings at a time; then a stake of a pound, and so on, and so on; Fardale, of course, should never have allowed a mere youngster to bet with him. But Fardale knew there was money behind me; still, when it came to owing him fifty-one pounds, he got nasty.

'Look here, young man,' he said, chancing to meet me in Ullathwaite market-place on that sixteenth day of October, 'you owe me fifty-one pounds. When are you going to pay up?'

I was not without a considerable share of self-assurance and what is called cheekiness in those days, and I answered him flippantly.

'When you owe me fifty-one pounds!' I retorted. 'Then we'll be square.'

He gave me a straight and sour look.

'Listen, my lad!' he said. 'I'm not going to be played with like this! When you back a winner, you want your money down on the nail——'

'Naturally!' I said, no doubt with impudence.

'And you get it,' he continued. 'I never owe money to my clients! But if you lose, after making a bet on credit, I can't get the money out of you. I've waited some time for you to settle up, and I shan't wait any longer. Pay up, my son, or take the consequences!'

I was still inclined to be defiant, and even rude.

'Look here, Fardale!' I said. 'Don't you bully me! Let me call your attention to the law. By the 8th and 9th Victoria, Chapter 109, it's enacted——'

'None of that, my lad!' he broke in, with a growl. 'I know the law about my own business as well as you do, and perhaps a good deal better. But there are ways and means outside the law. I'm a bit sick of you, young fellow, so I'll just tell you straight! You'll pay me my fifty-one pounds by eleven o'clock day after to-morrow, the 18th that'll be, or I shall call on your father, tell him all about it, and refuse any more business with you. And don't you forget that I'm a man of my word, and what I say I shall do, I shall do! I'm giving you forty-eight hours' grace to find the money, but if it isn't there—well, you'll see!'

He moved off, evidently in a nasty temper, before I could say anything, and I knew it was no good running after him to plead for mercy. I also knew that I had about as much prospect of finding fifty-one pounds in cash by eleven o'clock on the day after to-morrow as I had of being made President of the Law Society. All the available money I had in the world was three pounds, ten shillings—pocket-money intended to last me till the end of the half-quarter.

That Fardale should tell my father that I owed him fifty-one pounds as a betting debt was the last thing I desired. My father, though not so Puritanical as my mother, was a very strict man about certain things, and he detested gambling in any form. Moreover, if Fardale told my father, my father would tell my mother—and I knew what that would mean. Did Fardale really intend to carry out his threat? In my opinion he did.

What was to be done? Where and how was I to raise fifty-one pounds in forty-eight hours? I walked back to my father's office feeling very much upset. Before reaching there I met a friend of my youth, Jim Halstan: he buttonholed me.

'I say, old man!' he said. 'Have you got anything on to-morrow's three-thirty?'

'What is to-morrow's three-thirty?' I growled.

'Great Oakshire Handicap, you ass!' he exclaimed. 'Forgotten?'

'Clean!' said I. 'No!'

'Well, I've just had a special tip, old man,' he went on. 'Charlie Swann gave it me—he's had it from a chap that really is in the know. Heather Mixture, old man, is the tip!—dead cert! Look here!'

He pulled out a midday edition of a sporting paper and proceeded to show me the name of Heather Mixture in the list of entries for the race concerned. I shrugged my shoulders.

'Pooh!' I said scornfully. 'A rank outsider!'

'Never mind, old man!' he retorted. 'I had it from Charlie Swann, and Charlie had it from a man who knows something about the stable. Heather Mixture, my boy, will be there!'

'Have you backed it?' I asked.

'I have, old man. A fiver. With Sanderson, old man. Your man's Fardale, isn't he?'

'What did Sanderson give you?' I demanded, ignoring the last part of the question. 'It's at twenties here.'

'Sanderson, old man, gave me twenty-five,' he answered. 'Have a spec, old man—Charlie Swann——'

But I had nodded and turned away. Halstan did not know why, nor would I have told him. But just as he was speaking his last words, I, happening to glance over his shoulder, saw behind him the plate-glass window of a tailor's shop. In it, fixed in a roll of cloth, was a cardboard label, on which was boldly imprinted the words 'Heather Mixture.'

I went straight to a certain tavern in a quiet alley off the market-place where I knew I could find Sanderson. I caught him in a snug little parlour which at that moment he had all to himself: he looked at me with some surprise.

'Do anything for you, Mr Richard?' he asked.

'What price Heather Mixture?' I asked, without ceremony.

'To-morrow's three-thirty, eh?' he said. 'Ah, well—twenty, Mr Richard.'

'No!' I exclaimed. 'You gave Jim Halstan twenty-fives.'

'Aye, but it's shortening since then,' he answered. 'However, as it's the first time I've had the pleasure, Mr Richard—well, twenty-five, then. Cash, sir?'

I flung two sovereigns on the table before him and went away. If Heather Mixture won the Great Oakshire Handicap next day, I should be able to pay Fardale. If it didn't . . .

At three-forty-five the following afternoon, October 17, I got the result of the Great Oakshire Handicap. Heather Mixture, placed second, had lost by a short head.

3

I reflected, as I threw the paper aside, no doubt with a muttered curse, that Heather Mixture would have been more fitly named Forlorn Hope!—anyhow, the transaction had not only ruined my hope of paying Fardale, but had left me two pounds worse off than I was before interviewing his rival bookmaker, Sanderson. I was in the market-place again when I heard this unwelcome result of my speculation, and there again I met Halstan. He grinned all over his face at sight of me.

'What did I tell you?' he shouted. 'Didn't I say Heather Mixture would be there—or thereabouts?'

'You damned ass!' I snarled. 'Heather Mixture was second!'

'Isn't that thereabouts?' he retorted. 'Of course, you backed him both ways? I did!'

'Well, I didn't!' I said. 'I backed him to win.'

'Why didn't you back him both ways?' he persisted. 'I got one third the odds—so I'm all right. Why didn't you?'

I made no reply: it would have been no good telling him that I wanted fifty pounds and in wanting it had thought of nothing else. And I was sheering off, still cursing my bad luck, when he stopped me.

'Look here, old man!' he said. 'I know of another good thing—same source of information—for the first race, the one-thirty to-morrow. Flycatcher! I can get you fifteens off Sanderson. Dead cert, old man!'

I had thirty shillings in my pocket, of my own, and ten shillings which belonged to the office. I pulled out the two pounds and handed it over.

'All right—stick it on, then, with Sanderson, mind, nobody else—and both ways, this time,' I said. 'See you to-morrow afternoon, somewhere.'

I left Halstan then, and went on my way—I had something to do. And in telling what that something was, I shall introduce a matter which had a most important bearing on the catastrophe already close at hand, but all undreamed-of by me—or, I suppose, by anybody. The something was this. When I met Halstan I was on my way to the bookstall at Ullathwaite Railway Station: my business there was to collect three new novels which I had ordered some days before for Mrs Norrington. Mrs Norrington, usually resident in Ullathwaite, was just then staying in Harrogate: I had an appointment to meet her at Harrogate that very evening of October 17.

Mrs Norrington, like almost everybody concerned in this story, is dead now, and if she were alive she would not mind, *now*, that I write down all I am going to write down. So I shall tell all about her and myself, keeping nothing back.

Mrs Norrington, at the time of which I am telling, was a very pretty, vivacious woman of about twenty-eight or thirty—looking back on that time from my present standpoint of middle-age, I remember her as a very attractive woman. But she was married—I was going to say she had the bad luck to be married, though some people would have called it good luck having a view to material considerations—to a man who was some forty years older than herself. I never knew the real truth about that marriage: she scarcely ever mentioned her husband to me. But it was said that she had been a professional nurse, and that Mr Norrington, a very wealthy man, retired from business, and an invalid, had married her so that she could nurse him. And certainly from what I saw of their *ménage* she was more nurse and housekeeper than wife; Mr Norrington was always more or less ill, and when he was fit for any movement she had to cart him about to one health resort, in England or on the Continent, or another. Still, she did get some occasional relaxation, and during the winter of 1898-99 she took part in an amateur theatrical performance at Ullathwaite in which I also figured; that was how I made her acquaintance. I used to walk home with her after rehearsals and performances; after the theatricals were over we used to meet: I used to get books for her—perhaps we were in love with each other: I never really knew. But we did meet, openly at first; then secretly. There was a summer-house in the Norringtons' grounds where we often met, late at night. . . .

However, that is scarcely to the point of what is absolutely relevant to this account. What is relevant is that on the night of that 17th October I had an appointment to meet Mrs Norrington in Harrogate. She and her husband were staying at the United Empire Hotel there: I was to meet her at a certain place in the garden of the hotel at eight o'clock. Of course, no one was to know anything about this, and in order to put my own people clean off the scent I gave out that I was going over to spend the night with a friend of ours, Mr Verrill, at Lowsthorpe, some thirty miles away. What I really intended to do was to meet Mrs Norrington at Harrogate, and, after seeing her, go on to Lowsthorpe—I believe I had some sort of notion that I might tell Verrill my trouble about Fardale and get him to help me out of it. As things turned out, however, I never went to Lowsthorpe at all.

I made my preparations for setting out for Harrogate about six o'clock that evening, having previously mentioned, casually, that I was bound for Verrill's house at Lowsthorpe. Fetching my bicycle into our front hall, I strapped on the carrier the parcel of books which I had got that afternoon from the station bookstall, and, thinking that I might need it next morning, if, as was usual when I stayed with him, I went for a walk round his farm with Verrill, I also strapped on to the cross-bar a certain thick ash-plant stick which had a spud at the end. My sister Audrey came into the hall while I was making these preparations, and, woman-like, began to ask inquisitive questions.

'What's in that parcel, Dick?' she demanded.

'What's that got to do with you?' I retorted, brother-like.

'It's books!' she said, handling the parcel. 'Are you taking them to Verrill's? Are they novels? Because, if they are, you might have let me read them first.'

'You read quite enough novel stuff as it is!' said I. 'You're always fetching novels home. And who said they were novels—how do you know they aren't law-books, eh?'

'I guess they aren't!' she retorted. 'Catch you carting law-books off when you're away for the night! I don't believe they're for Verrill, either. You're going to leave them with some girl or other, my lad!'

'Have it your own way!' said I. 'And if you want something useful to do, miss, tell the pater I shall go straight to the office in the morning.'

Then I went off, and presently, getting outside the town, went away towards Harrogate, where I duly arrived in good time for my appointment with Mrs Norrington. It was not the first meeting we had had there. The United Empire Hotel stands in large grounds in a quiet part of the town: there was an alcove, or arbour, in the grounds which made an admirable meeting-place after dark. And in its shelter at eight o'clock that night Mrs Norrington and I met. Neither of us knew it at the moment, but as a matter of fact we were meeting for the last time; after that night we never saw each other again.

During the whole of that ride to Harrogate I was thinking over my difficulty of the morrow. I felt no doubt about the reality of Fardale's threat. If I didn't pay up by eleven o'clock next morning he would certainly tell my father. Now, as I said before, my father was a very strict—and in my opinion a very strait-laced—man, and he abominated gambling. Also, being a man of position in the town, and Mayor of the Borough, he would be furiously angry to know that his son owed money; neither I nor my sister Audrey was allowed to contract debts. What my father would do, I reckoned, would be to pay Fardale, and then to dock me of a certain amount of my monthly allowance until the fifty-one pounds was paid off—a prospect which did not commend itself. Yet I saw little prospect of being able to raise the money myself. I had some notion of appealing to Verrill, who was a bit of a sport, but I knew that Verrill, who was at that time dabbling in amateur farming and not doing over-well at it, might not have fifty-one pounds at his command. That was a mere straw to clutch at—and there was no other. I dared not approach my mother—if my father was a bit strait-laced and particular, she was ten times more so; the mere news that I had been betting on horses would have horrified her. When everything was reckoned up it was plain that I was in for a bad time.

I suppose Mrs Norrington quickly gathered the fact that I was in the doldrums as soon as we met in the little summer-house of the hotel gardens. She came to me there wrapped in a big cloak, and her first words were to tell me that she couldn't stay long, for there was a dance on that night, and she was helping in managing it.

'But what's the matter, Dick?' she asked, breaking off suddenly in her talk about the dance. 'You're in the dumps to-night? Aren't you, now?'

To cut the story short, I told her all about it.

'Do you think Fardale means what he said?' she inquired. 'Or was it just a mere threat?'

'Fardale meant it all right,' said I. 'He's a nasty chap to get across with. And I dare say I cheeked him a bit. Oh, he'll split right enough. And then there'll be a hell of a row!'

'With your father?' she asked.

'And mother too,' I replied. 'I shall get it hot and strong.'

She was silent for a moment; then she gave my arm a squeeze.

'Dick,' she said, 'I've got some money, put away—but the thing is—how to get at it?'

'What do you mean?' I asked. 'Besides, I'm not going to take your money to pay Fardale!'

'You'll take it to avoid getting into an unpleasant mess, my dear!' she retorted. 'You must take it—of course you'll take it! But the thing is—how to get hold of it?'

'Again, what do you mean?' I inquired. 'Not that I intend taking it!'

'You'll just do what I say, Dick,' she answered. 'Now listen: how much does Fardale want? Exactly.'

'Fifty-one pounds,' I replied.

'I haven't got fifty-one pounds,' she said. 'But I've got forty-five in banknotes. Could you raise the other six?'

'I might,' I answered. 'But——'

'No buts,' she interrupted. 'You're going to have the forty-five—if we can get at the banknotes!'

'What's that mean?' I asked. 'Are they——?'

'Listen!' she said. 'I've got forty-five pounds in banknotes in a drawer of my dressing-table at home, in the house at Ullathwaite. But how are we to get at them? Here we are in Harrogate!'

'Give it up!' said I. 'You can't. Besides——'

'No!' she exclaimed. 'I know! Look here! I have a latch-key for the garden-door of the house—it's only on the latch. If I get that for you from my room in the hotel you can go back to Ullathwaite, go to the house, get the notes, and pay Fardale. Nobody will know. And the other six——'

'Forty-five would settle Fardale,' I said. 'But I don't want——'

'That's what we're going to do, Dick,' she interrupted, firmly. 'Be a good boy and obey orders. Now listen again—I'll get you the latch-key, and the key of the drawer in which the banknotes will be found in a little leather case, black morocco. My room is the first you come to on the first landing—first door on the right-hand side. The dressing-table is between the windows—the drawer is the top right-hand one. Do you think you can get into the house unobserved?'

'Do you really wish me to do this?' I asked.

'I do!—to please me,' she answered. 'And to please me you'll do something else, Dick. Don't bet again!—at any rate, until it's your own money that you bet with. You shouldn't bet with money that's taken from your father's allowance to you. Don't you see that?'

'Never saw it before,' I said. 'All right—I promise! It's a rotten game, anyhow. But I don't like——'

She was off down the garden before I could finish. Within a few minutes she was back, and as soon as she rejoined me she slipped two keys, tied together with a bit of ribbon, into my hand.

'There!' she said. 'That's all right! Settle with Fardale—and keep your promise. And now I've only got ten minutes to spare, Dick, so let's forget Fardale and all the nasty things.'

I think the ten minutes lengthened into fifteen, perhaps twenty. Certainly we forgot Fardale and everything else. And when we had said good-bye, and I was speeding off towards Ullathwaite again, I remembered that I had forgotten something else—I hadn't given her the parcel of new novels! Never mind—they would form an excuse for going over again. But I never went again—as I have already said, that was the last time that Irene Norrington and I ever met.

4

There was now no need for me to go on to Verrill's, and I occupied myself during the ride back to Ullathwaite in considering how I could get into the Norringtons' house unobserved. The house itself was one of certain modern residences which stood in a valley beneath the hill along the ridge of which Hagsdene Wood stretched; it, with the neighbouring houses, was reached from the town by a road that continued into the country. I dared not approach the house by that road, which was probably patrolled at some hour of the evening by a police-constable; I should have to gain it by some secret way. Fortunately, I knew well enough how to do that: all that was necessary was to do what I had often done when I had an appointment with Mrs Norrington, namely, to approach by way of Hagsdene Wood and the meadows that ran down the sloping hillside to the little stream which bordered the Norringtons' grounds. Nobody was likely to see me in the wood or on the meadows at that time of night. Nevertheless, in order to make the hour as late as possible, I took my time in returning, and it was just striking ten o'clock by Ullathwaite Town Hall when I dismounted from my machine at a gate which gave entrance to the wood.

I had made all my plans before reaching that gate, and was going to do what I had done many a time—leave my bicycle hidden just within the wood, cross the wood, go down the slopes, and make the Norringtons' house and its garden-door through the grounds. This I proceeded to carry out. I took from my bicycle the parcel of books which I had forgotten to leave with Mrs Norrington, and the ash-plant stick that I had fastened on the cross-bar when I left home, and with these in either hand struck out by a narrow path across the wood. It came out at my trial that these proceedings were watched by two people who were sweethearting there in the wood, Jim Collier and Ellen Hopkinson; their evidence was quite correct. But if they had followed me they would have seen that I went straight past the spot where Maidment's dead body was found next morning, passed the hedge of Hebb's cottage at the fringe of the wood, and went off down the meadows beyond. Also, if they had followed to where I went, they would have been able to testify that when the Town Hall clock next struck—at a quarter past ten—I was in the Norringtons' garden, cautiously creeping towards the house. I heard the quarter strike as I stood in the shelter of a clump of bushes, wondering if there was anybody about in the neighbouring gardens. Now, according to other evidence given at the trial, Maidment did not leave Hagsdene Park until a quarter past ten, and it would take him quite twenty minutes to walk from there to the place in the wood where he was found dead, next morning.

Everything was very quiet round the Norringtons' house, but as I was about to approach the door which communicated between it and the gardens I heard the click of the entrance gates on the opposite side of the grounds—the gates which opened on the road from the town. I knew well enough what that click meant. It meant that the policeman whose beat this was, knowing that the occupants were away and the house empty, was taking a look round. I hastily retreated into the bushes and hid myself as securely as possible. I hoped he wouldn't be very particular; if he shone his bull's-eye lantern here, there, and everywhere, he might detect me. I heard him pottering about at the front of the house for some time; then he came round to the back, and eventually to the side. From my hiding-place I saw him shine his light on the door I wanted, and on one or two windows close by; he was so careful and painstaking in his inspection that he then went down the garden and examined the summer-house. Eventually he went away, just as the half-hour chimed from the town—I have often thought since that had he discovered me he would have been the most useful witness my counsel could have brought forward in my behalf.

I waited another good quarter of an hour before I approached the side-door with the key which Mrs Norrington had given me. Once inside the house, with the door again locked from within, the silence and darkness were somewhat disconcerting: if it had been an old house I should have been nervous. And, knowing that the policeman was still somewhere in the neighbourhood, I dared not strike a match; to think of lighting any lamp or candle I came across was utterly out of the question. All I could do was to feel my way about—fortunately, I had been in the house before, more than once, and remembered its arrangements pretty accurately. And, making my way upstairs, and into the bedroom indicated, I very soon found the dressing-table, and the drawer, and the black morocco case and its contents—with a savage delight in thinking of Fardale's surprise when I flung his money in his face next morning.

And now there was the night to get over. But I had already settled what I would do about that. I felt for the bed. It had been dismantled, but there were blankets carefully folded at its foot, and an eider-down quilt. Throwing off nothing but the Norfolk jacket I was wearing, and kicking off my shoes, I wrapped a blanket round me, pulled the eider-down over me, and in five minutes was fast asleep. When I awoke there was a grey light stealing in through the windows on either side of the dressing-table. I had not forgotten to wind up my watch, and the light, when I went to the windows, was strong enough to show me that the time was seven o'clock. It was also strong enough—without any drawing up of the blinds—to enable me to count the banknotes. There they were, exactly as Mrs Norrington had said—nine £5 Bank of England notes. Forty-five pounds!—and I was still six pounds short. But I had already settled as to how I was to get that amount.

The next thing was to get out of the house as quietly and secretly as I had entered it. Also I had to regain my bicycle. I have already said that I had brought the parcel of books and my ash-plant stick into the house. The books I left in Mrs Norrington's bedroom, on a table by the bed; she would find them when she returned home. As for the ash-plant, I had put it down in a corner of the hall when I came in; when I went out that morning I forgot it. I had a more important thing to think about—and that was, how to get to the gate on the other side of the wood, and to regain my machine there, without being seen. There might be men about in the wood—woodmen, gamekeepers, labourers taking a short cut. And, most dangerous of all, there was Hebb's cottage. Its windows on one side overlooked the meadows on the slope of the hill; on another, the path that led from near the Norringtons' house to the fringe of the wood. And if Hebb and his wife, or either of them, happened to be up early and to be looking out, I should be seen.

However, being pretty ingenious, I got over these difficulties easily enough. Having made sure, as far as I could, that there was nobody about, front, back, or side, I let myself out of the house by the garden-door, put the key in my pocket, and slipped away through the bushes to the edge of the little stream at the end of the grounds. There was a narrow path along its banks, shaded by dwarf trees: I made my way along this for some distance, until I reached a plantation of fir and larch on the hillside and became completely sheltered in it. Making my way through this up the hill, I struck Hagsdene Wood at a point well beyond Hebb's cottage, and, making a *détour* thence, went right round the far extent of the wood, and so came to where I had left the bicycle. Taking it out of the bushes in which I had hidden it the previous evening, I lifted it into the lane, and, mounting the saddle, rode off towards the town.

But I was not going home. It was nearly eight o'clock by that time, and I knew that Mrs Sallitt, the woman who acted as caretaker at our offices and lived in the basement, would be up. And up she was, and sweeping at the entrance-hall when I walked in with my bicycle.

'Lawk-a-massy, Mr Richard!' she exclaimed at sight of me. 'You give me quite a turn when I see you a-jumping off that there bike! But then you and your pa is such queer 'uns for hours!—your pa was here last night till I dunno what time this morning. What they calls the small hours, anyhow.'

There was nothing surprising to me in that bit of news. During his term as Mayor of Ullathwaite my father had had so many duties and matters to attend to that his own professional work often got into arrears, and to clear these off he often went to his office late in the evening, after he had dined, and stayed there, working, by himself until after midnight.

'Oh, he was here last night, was he, Mrs Sallitt?' I said. 'And late?'

'Which he come in as me and Sallitt was just going to bed, about half-past eleven o'clock it would be, Master Richard,' she answered. 'I hear his latch-key, and I says to Sallitt, I says, "That'll be the Mayor!" I says. "Go up and see if there's anything he wants." Which Sallitt did, immediate. But there wasn't nothing he wanted but a jug of cold water and for me and Sallitt to go to bed. Which we proceeds to do, Master Richard, but me sleeping light hears your pa go away and the Town Hall clock strike symultaneous, as they calls it.'

'Oh!' I said, not particularly interested. 'Well, look here, Mrs Sallitt, do you think you could get me a nice cup of tea, and some bread and butter? I've had a long ride, and I don't want to go home to breakfast—I've some work to do here before anybody comes.'

Mrs Sallitt was agreeable; she produced the tea and bread and butter very speedily and brought it into my room. And when I had refreshed myself I went, first into my father's private room, and then into the clerks' room—I had something to do before Hebb and the other clerks and the office-boy arrived.

There were signs in my father's room that he had been there, and they were unusual. An empty whisky bottle stood on his desk, and near it the jug of water of which Mrs Sallitt had spoken, flanked by a single glass. Now it was a very uncommon thing, in my experience, that my father drank whisky at all; he liked a glass of good port, but he seldom touched spirits; in this case, however, he must have had two or three good strong glasses of whisky, for I remembered that on the previous afternoon I, by his orders, had given a glass of whisky to an old gentleman who had called on business, and I recollected the amount left in the bottle when I restored it to its place in a cupboard by the fireside. I put the empty bottle back in that cupboard now, wondering. But that was not what I wanted. What I did want was to know how much loose cash there was lying in a certain drawer in the clerks' office—a drawer of which my father had one key, I another, and our managing clerk, Hebb, a third. This money was kept there for current expenses and payments; sometimes there was a good deal there; sometimes only a small sum: anything that was paid in, in cash, was thrown into that drawer, and from it weekly or daily disbursements were made.

There was a good deal of money in the drawer that morning—cheques, banknotes, postal orders, silver, gold; more gold than usual. I took out six sovereigns, scarcely glancing at them, and, leaving the question of how and when I was to replace them to some other time, I put these six sovereigns in my pocket along with Mrs Norrington's forty-five pounds. Now I had the wherewithal for freeing myself of Fardale. And I felt very cock-a-whoop about it—Fardale, I said to myself, should have a piece of my mind.

Everybody was late in arriving at the office that morning. At ten o'clock nobody had come but a youngster of about my own age, Witherspoon, who was articled to my father, and the office-boy: Hebb, our managing clerk, who was usually at his desk by nine-thirty, had not come at ten minutes past ten, when I went out. Neither had my father—but that was no matter of surprise; his mayoral duties often took him to the Town Hall before he could get to the office.

I went off to Fardale's, with my fifty-one pounds in my pocket. Fardale lived in a rather far-off corner of the town. He'd gone out for a few minutes, they said, when I reached his house, so I walked about outside. There was a newsagent's shop at the corner; I went in and bought a sporting paper and was very much astonished to see that the horse I had backed for that afternoon had considerably shortened in price. While I was wondering if it had any real chance and would be worth backing further, Fardale came along; I could see that he was surprised to find me awaiting him.

I pulled out the banknotes and the six sovereigns, all lumped together, and shoved them at him.

'There's your money, Mr Fardale,' I said in as lordly a fashion as I could command. 'And it's the last of mine you'll ever see. You don't know how to treat a gentleman!'

Without troubling to look at or count them, he thrust the notes and gold into a pocket of his trousers, looking at me coolly.

'No?' he said quietly. 'It's the first complaint I've had!'

'There are other bookmakers than you in the town,' I said.

'Several,' he answered. 'But none so ready to accommodate young fellows with credit.'

'Well, I shall go elsewhere in future,' I said, chafing at his coolness. 'I'm not going to be threatened by anybody.'

He smiled a little at that.

'Look here, my lad!' he said. 'You're young, and you're green, and no doubt you think men like me roll in money. But I'll spout you some lines that an old fellow spouted to me, long since: I've never forgotten 'em!—

It's a very good world that we live in
To spend, and to lend, and to give in;
But to beg, or to borrow, or get a man's own,
It's the very worst world that ever was known!

I find it difficult to get my own sometimes, my lad—and so I have to ask for it, sharply. Good morning!'

He turned on his heel and moved off towards his house, and I went away feeling rather small. However, Fardale was paid. But I was owing six pounds to the cash-box at the office. Well, perhaps I should have a bit of luck that afternoon, and anyhow I needn't repay the six pounds before the end of the week.

When I got back to the office Hebb had arrived. He was taking off his overcoat as I entered. He gave me an inquiring look.

'Heard the news, Mr Richard?' he asked.

'Heard nothing,' said I. 'What news?'

'You know that chap Maidment, the rent-collector?' he continued.

'Just know that there is such a fellow,' I answered. 'What of him?'

'Found dead in Hagsdene Wood this morning,' he replied. 'Close by my house. And there's no doubt he was murdered. And robbed, too!'

'Any clue?' I asked.

'They haven't anything much to go on so far,' he said. 'Henderson's busy about it, of course. There's no doubt he was tricked, Maidment. He'd been collecting rents at that new property at Hagsdene Park, and they say he'd have about a hundred pounds or rather more on him. Hadn't a penny of it when his body was found! Of course, he'd been knocked on the head for it.'

'And near your place?' I asked.

'Within a very few yards,' he answered. 'But we never heard anything—not a sound. To be sure, I wasn't at home about the time they think it occurred, but my wife was, and she never heard anything.'

'What time did it occur?' I inquired.

'The doctors think about half-past ten or a quarter to eleven,' he replied. 'I don't know how they fix it, but that's what they say. Last night, anyway, it was. Dead for hours when he was found.'

We went on to further talk: the murder was, of course, the main topic of conversation everywhere in Ullathwaite that morning. I had no opportunity of discussing it with my father; he was out, at the Town Hall. But just after lunch I got a telephone call from him, telling me to go over to him at the Mayor's Parlour. I went there at once—to find Henderson, the Police Superintendent, with him.

5

I have a vivid recollection, even at this length of time, of how the mere sight of Henderson not only put me on my guard, but also gave me an idea of why he was there and what was coming. Certain things flashed through my mind at once. Maidment had been murdered in Hagsdene Wood the night before. I had been in Hagsdene Wood the night before. Maidment had been robbed of the money he carried about him. That morning I had been in possession of money. But who knew but Fardale? Why should Fardale give that fact away? Had he given it away? If so, why? Anyhow, Henderson was there closeted with my father, and both were regarding me with strange, questioning glances. Swift as lightning came the thought that Mrs Norrington was in danger, and just as swift my resolution to say nothing, admit nothing that could bring her name into question.

Within one minute of my entrance to the Mayor's Parlour I had made two admissions: one, that I had not spent the night with Verrill at Lowsthorpe; the other, that I had paid money to Fardale that morning. Then came something that caused me absolute astonishment—Henderson subsequently admitted that my astonishment was obvious and genuine. He said that among the six sovereigns which I had paid to Fardale there was one which was marked—a coin through which somebody, at some time, had drilled a small hole: he said, too, that he had proof that this sovereign had been paid to Maidment the night before by a man named Collingwood, a tenant at Hagsdene Park, and the presumption was that Maidment's murderer had taken it, with other money, from his victim's pocket. And now Henderson wanted to know how I had got hold of it before paying it to Fardale?

I did some quick thinking then. As I have already said, I took six sovereigns out of this drawer in our clerks' office that morning, in order to make up my full amount of fifty-one pounds, but I never looked particularly at the coins; certainly I had never seen the perforated sovereign. But I wasn't going to tell Henderson where I had got the six sovereigns: I wanted time to think. And deliberately assuming a sullen and defiant air I refused to say anything, and I went away slamming the door behind me, as if I were highly incensed at even the suggestion of an accusation.

But once outside the Mayor's Parlour I began to think in a very serious fashion. I knew Collingwood: he was a decent, highly respectable man. I knew Fardale; in spite of his recent drastic treatment of me he was honest and straightforward. It was possible that I had paid him the very sovereign, marked by perforation, which Collingwood had paid Maidment, and had subsequently been removed from Maidment's dead body. But in that case, *how had that sovereign come to be in our office drawer*?

I stood at the corner of the market-place a while, deeply absorbed in this question. Maidment, according to the account I had received, had been murdered about half-past ten o'clock the previous evening. Presumably he had been robbed of all the money he had on him a few minutes later. Well, again the question came up—if that marked sovereign was among the money, how came it to be in our office next morning?

Suddenly a thought, a name, flashed into my mind. Hebb! Was Hebb the murderer and the thief?

I began to reckon things up:

1. Hebb's cottage was close by the scene of the murder.
2. Hebb and Maidment might have met and quarrelled.
3. Hebb had a key to our office-door—the outer door. He could admit himself to the office at any hour of the day or night.
4. Hebb—supposing that he was the murderer and thief—might have remembered that we had money in notes and gold lying in our office drawer and have thought that it would be to his advantage to exchange it for his plunder. He would know that he ran little risk of discovery in visiting the office either during the night or very early in the morning.
5. Anyway, if the perforated sovereign which Fardale asserted I had handed to him was really the same coin that Collingwood had paid to Maidment, it had come into my hands from our cash-drawer. *How had it got there? Who put it there, between 10.30 the previous evening and 8.30 next morning?*

Taking it altogether, I thought Hebb a very likely man to fix on. I knew him to be a shifty, underhand sneak, and had often wondered why my father retained his services. Very likely, it was Hebb. But I knew this much—I was not going to voice my thoughts. Let Henderson do his own work.

As I stood there, reflecting, Sanderson, the bookmaker, came along. He had a telegram in his hand and waved it at me. I had completely forgotten the commission I had entrusted to Halstan the day before and I wondered what Sanderson was smiling at.

'You've struck it this time, young man!' he said. 'Lose one day, win another, what?'

He shoved the bit of flimsy pink paper into my hand, and I stared at it, scarcely comprehending.

1 Flycatcher, 2 Red Nose, 3 Silly Betty.

'Oh?' I said, still a bit muddled. 'So Flycatcher won, eh?'

'So it seems,' he replied, dryly. 'I gave you fifteen to one, and one third the odds a place, so you want—let's see—you want twenty-two quid, Mr Richard. Give it you now, if you like.'

'I should make no objections, Mr Sanderson, thank you,' I replied. 'And—er, if you've got a few sovereigns?'

He drew me aside into a narrow passage and handed over twelve sovereigns and two five-pound notes. I thanked him and went away—back to the office.

The clerks' office was empty. Hebb was out somewhere. I heard the office-boy, a lazy young scamp, gossiping in the basement with Mrs Sallitt. Witherspoon was in a room upstairs which he and I shared. So I did what I wanted to do—which was to open the cash-drawer and replace the equivalent of the six sovereigns I had taken from it that morning. That put the cash right. The drawer and its contents had apparently not been touched since I had opened it earlier in the day.

I saw nothing of my father all that afternoon; nothing, indeed, until I went home at the close of the day's business: I did not meet him, in fact, until our dinner-hour arrived. While he, my mother, my sister Audrey, and myself were dining, our parlourmaid announced Colonel Patterson, the Chief Constable, and Henderson, the Police Superintendent. My father had a private conversation with them in his study; then they came into the dining-room, and Patterson made an appeal to me to speak. I took up the attitude I had adopted at the Mayor's Parlour, and they went away.

We finished dinner in silence. When the parlourmaid had finally retired, and we four were left to ourselves, my father spoke.

'Now, Dick,' he said, 'those fellows will come back. They'll come for you! Before they come, let us four have a quiet talk.'

6

I was not particularly inclined to take part in any family conference, but I held my tongue and let my father have his way. And it was his way, as a formal and practical man, to start out by asking me four questions.

'Now, Dick,' he began, 'I want to ask you certain things, in the presence of your mother and your sister. We shall all rely on your telling us the truth. And to start with—are you responsible, in any way, for Maidment's death?'

'No!' I replied firmly. 'Absolutely not!'

'Had you anything to do with robbing his dead body?' he asked.

'Nothing!' I answered.

'Will you tell me where you got the money which you handed over to Fardale?' he continued.

'No!' I said, more firmly than ever. 'I can't!'

'Will you say where you spent last night?' he concluded.

'I can't tell you that either,' I replied. 'Sorry—but I can't answer either of the last two questions.'

He nodded his head as if I had said exactly what he had expected I should say. My mother spoke.

'Surely you can tell us, Dick!' she urged.

'No, Mother, I can't tell anyone,' I said. 'That's final!'

My father got up from the table, and, going over to a cigar cabinet which stood at the corner of the mantelpiece, selected and lighted a cigar.

'Well,' he said, after a pause, 'we may as well face things! They'll come for you, Dick. To-night, I expect.'

My mother and Audrey let out exclamations; I said nothing.

'Do you really mean that, John?' asked my mother.

'I mean it!' he said. 'I don't see how they can avoid it. That marked sovereign! And Dick's being seen in Hagsdene Wood and other circumstances. Well, we shall have to go through with it!'

'But—but will they take him away?' asked my mother.

'They'll take me away and lock me up for the night, and stick me before the magistrates to-morrow morning, Mother,' I said as cheerfully as I could. 'And their worships will send me to the Assizes at Grandminster, to be tried before a judge and jury. And the jury will return a verdict of "Not Guilty." '

'Suppose they don't?' said Audrey.

'Fools if they don't!' I retorted. 'I'm not afraid, anyhow.'

'There are usually some fools on a jury,' remarked my father. 'It all depends on how things are put before them. I shall get Wilsborough to represent you before the magistrates, and if they do send you for trial we will get the best counsel we can.'

'John!' exclaimed my mother. 'You talk as if—as if it were somebody else, instead of its being Dick!'

'Unfortunately it is Dick,' said my father. 'I take Dick's word that he is absolutely innocent. But I am bound to say, as a solicitor, not without some appreciation of the value of evidence, that the case as it has presented itself to the police is suspicious. Dick's obstinate silence——'

'Why won't you speak, Dick!' interrupted my mother. 'Surely——'

'Dick's obstinate silence,' continued my father, waving his hand, 'will be taken as confirmatory of his guilt. Personally, I feel quite sure as to the development of the affair. I agree with Dick that he will be acquitted. I have heard Henderson's presentation of the case for the prosecution. It is not strong enough. I don't believe any jury would find a verdict of guilty on such evidence. Still, you never know. Juries are more or less swayed by what a judge says. But if Dick were found guilty——'

'Oh, don't!' said my mother. 'Don't suggest——'

'If Dick were found guilty,' continued my father, 'I have every confidence that the verdict would be set aside by the Home Secretary. As I say, the evidence—at any rate such evidence as has been put together by Henderson——'

I rose from my chair at this point; my father was apt to become long-winded and prosy if he got discussing legal matters.

'Where are you going, Dick?' asked my mother, anxiously.

'To put a few things together, Mother,' I replied. 'I suppose I can take a toothbrush and similar necessities, and I may as well be ready.'

She threw up her hands with a gesture of despair and applied her handkerchief to her eyes. I left the room, and Audrey followed me out, and in the hall outside laid a hand on my arm.

'Dick!' she said, pleadingly. 'Can't you tell me—just me?'

'Not even you, Audrey!' I answered. 'Just you!'

'I know what you're after,' she went on. 'You're shielding somebody!'

'Not Maidment's murderer, anyway!' I said. 'Make yourself sure about that.'

'No—but somebody!' she persisted. 'And just think what danger you're in!'

'Frankly, I don't think I am,' I replied. 'The whole thing seems like a cock-and-bull story to me—I mean, what Henderson can bring against me. I know nothing about the murder or the robbery.'

'But—the marked coin?' she said. 'That——'

'Good Lord, how's Fardale going to prove that I even gave him a marked coin?' I exclaimed. 'How can he swear, I mean, that the coin I gave him is the identical coin paid to Maidment by Collingwood? Sovereigns with holes in them aren't uncommon—lots of men carry one on their watch-chains.'

'But—but the disgrace and discomfort of being arrested!' she said. 'And being kept in a prison cell——'

'Fortunately it's winter, so there's no cricket to miss, I said lightly. 'And I believe prisoners on remand are treated pretty much as if they were in a decent hotel. No good bothering, Audrey, it's got to be gone through. It'll soon be over.'

She stared at me a minute. Then her eyes suddenly widened.

'Oh, well,' she said. 'I'll see what I can do. But, Dick—have you any idea who did murder Maidment? Have you, now?'

I thought for a moment. Then I made up my mind.

'No!' I said. 'I haven't. The whole thing's a mystery. And that I should be suspected is just due to a series of remarkable coincidences.'

I left her at that, and, going up to my room, packed a small suitcase with necessities. I had no doubt that the local magistrates would commit me for trial; already, in my brief experience of the Law, I had known examples of their unwillingness to decide things for themselves.

When I went downstairs again the police were awaiting me. I went away with them.

7

I was duly committed for trial, as I had expected, and in due course I made my appearance in the dock at Grandminster Assizes. Although my life was at stake I felt all through the trial as if I were a spectator. I had a strong counsel, Henshawe, Q.C., and I am sure he did his best. Yet the Judge seemed to sum up against me: I believe he viewed with great disfavour my obstinacy in refusing to give evidence, as I might have done under the new Criminal Evidence

Act which had recently become law. And as spectator this is how I summed things up—I mean, this is how they presented themselves to me:

1. The prosecution put forward the theory that the money I paid to Fardale was the proceeds of the robbery of Maidment's dead body.

But the notes—Bank of England notes—which I handed to Fardale were, as the evidence showed, not the notes which Maidment had collected from certain of the Hagsdene Park tenants.

2. The prosecution alleged that a certain perforated sovereign which I gave to Fardale among six that made up the payment of fifty-one pounds was the identical coin paid by Collingwood to Maidment.

But—as even the Judge himself remarked in the course of his summing-up—sovereigns with holes in them were not uncommon, and in spite of Fardale's assertion it was possible that when I gave him the six pounds in gold he already had a sovereign so marked in his pocket.

3. The prosecution suggested that a certain oak stick, a cheap shilling walking-stick, common as blackberries, found concealed in Hagsdene Wood, near the scene of the murder, and believed to be the weapon with which Maidment had been struck down, was my property and had been taken to the wood by me on my bicycle.

But my sister Audrey was able to swear that the stick which she saw me fasten on the cross-bar of my machine when I was leaving my father's house on the evening of October 17 was an ash-plant stick, and a man who sold sticks in Ullathwaite, Shillaker, scorned, on oath, the idea that anyone could tell any cheap oak stick, stained yellow, from another.

However, I got a surprise when the last stages of the trial arrived. His lordship, who, as I have said, seemed to regard me and my attitude of silence with such disfavour, summed up against me—at least, he appeared to. Still, I never believed that the jury would trouble to leave their box—I thought they would decide in my favour at once. But they retired! And at the end of an hour, they were still in retirement—and at the end of two hours—and at the end of three, and four, and five . . .

It was very late in the evening when they fetched me up from the cells to hear the verdict. It was just what I had expected—*Not Guilty*. But why had the jury been so long in arriving at it? Then I remembered that I, and I alone, knew a lot of things that they didn't know.

I paid no attention to the congratulations which poured in on me. What I was thinking was that, in spite of everything, I had kept intact my secret and Mrs Norrington's.

8

As soon as the trial was over I joined my father, mother, and sister, and we returned to Ullathwaite. From the moment in which I rejoined them—my father in the court, my mother and Audrey at an hotel close by—the Maidment affair was never again mentioned in our home circle.

I resumed my work at the office next day as if nothing had happened. I knew, of course, that there were people in the town and neighbourhood who still suspected me and always would suspect me. I determined to pay no attention to anything that might be said or that I might hear. As a matter of fact I don't remember that anyone ever did mention these matters to me—with the exception of Hebb. Hebb approached me the day after the trial, looking very sheepish.

'I was very sorry to have to give that evidence about the stick, Mr Richard,' he said, in an unnecessarily apologetic manner. 'But those police chaps had me on toast, you know!'

'How did they have you on toast?' I asked, no doubt a little sneeringly. 'I never heard of it.'

'Well, you see,' he answered, 'Henderson came across me in Hagsdene Wood, suddenly, the evening they'd been searching there. He stuck that oak stick right in front of me, asking if I knew anything of it or had ever seen it. And upon my honour I did think it was the stick I'd given you! I'd no idea sticks of that sort were as common as they are—Shillaker's evidence was a surprise to me. And you see, when I'd once said what I had to Henderson I had to stand by it. My mistake, of course!'

'Might have been a pretty expensive mistake for me!' I remarked.

'I know—I know!' he said contritely. 'But, you see, I didn't attach such importance to it at the time. And when I first saw it, I did honestly think it was the stick I'd given you.'

I made no further answer: I wasn't going to discuss recent events with Hebb. And before very long Hebb was removed out of my reach. He and his wife suddenly left Ullathwaite. Hebb, just before the Maidment affair, had qualified as a solicitor, and within a few weeks of my trial I heard that he had got a partnership in a firm in a small town in the south-west of England, some four hundred miles away, and was going to leave my father's employ. It is not necessary to say here how I found out the fact, but this partnership was bought for Hebb by my father. So Hebb and his pretty wife vanished from Ullathwaite—and at times, when my mind turned back to October 1899, I wondered . . . but I was never quite certain as to what it was that I wondered.

I settled down to my work. I had done a lot of thinking while awaiting my trial. One thing I had resolved on—I would do no more betting. I had promised Mrs Norrington, and I meant to keep the promise. But I had no opportunity of telling her that I was keeping it. I had sent her keys back to her at the Harrogate hotel the morning after making use of them, but from the moment of my arrest to that of my acquittal I neither heard from nor of her. Just after the trial I heard that she and her husband had left England for Egypt. But she never wrote to me. I heard nothing of her until some months later; then I heard—saw, rather, in *The Times*—that Mr Norrington was dead. I thought she would write then. But she didn't. And the next thing I learned—from another announcement in *The Times*—was that she had married again, at some place on the Riviera. So—there was an end of that.

And again I went on with my work. In pursuance of the usual custom, I served one year of my articles with our London agents; after completing that I passed my examinations and became a full-fledged and duly qualified solicitor of the High Court. And then my father took me into partnership, and the big brass plate on the office door showed the style and title of Radford & Radford.

From the time of my trial onward my father showed me a consideration and, in his somewhat frigid way, an affection which I had never received from him previously. He increased my allowance considerably; he began to consult me about things; we became more of friends. This intimacy between us deepened, first when my mother died; again, still more, when Audrey married and went off with her bridegroom to the Antipodes. During the last years of his life my father and I were very close friends; all the closer because I myself never married. And when he in his turn died he left me everything he had—Audrey had been provided for in very handsome fashion on her marriage.

And my father left me something else in addition to all his real and personal estate. In a certain deed-box, the key of which he carried securely attached to his watch-chain, I found a sealed envelope, containing what was evidently some bulky document, and endorsed in my father's handwriting:

> *For my son, Richard Radford, to be opened by him after my Death.*

I let some days elapse before I broke the seal of this envelope. Then, one night, locking myself in the study, I spread the contents of the package before me and read what my father had written.

9

Contents of the Sealed Packet

Ullathwaite, March 15, 1924

Being informed by my medical advisers that—in consequence of a certain internal complaint from which I have suffered for some time—the duration of my life cannot be extended many months, I feel it incumbent upon me to set down, while I have the power to do so, a true statement as regards the facts and happenings of October 17, 1899, which resulted in the trial for murder of my son Richard. No other living person than myself knows the real truth about that unfortunate affair: no other person, indeed, ever has known it, though two persons may have made guesses at it. Whether my son ever guessed it I do not know; he passed through his ordeal in silence, and successfully. He will read this when I am dead, and will learn from what I have to say why, during that time of trial, I held my peace. If my silence caused him trouble and anxiety—as it inevitably must have done—I have endeavoured to compensate him for it a thousandfold, and I feel sure that when this has been read by him he will have no hard thought of me for the reticence which I was compelled to adopt.

Now in beginning let me repeat what I have already said. I am the only person in the world who knows, and who ever did know, the absolute truth about the so-called murder of Roger Maidment in Hagsdene Wood near Ullathwaite in October 1899. I now proceed to tell in plain, straightforward fashion, why I did not tell the truth at the time.

In 1899 I had in my office at Ullathwaite a managing clerk named Hebb. He was at that time a young man of about thirty years of age. He had worked his way up from being a mere office-boy to becoming a qualified solicitor. He was married to a very pretty young wife, of a class somewhat superior to his own; she was in her way a clever little woman and had ambition for her husband: I should say, from my recollection of the two, that in brain-power she excelled Hebb, whose chief characteristic—an admirable one, to be sure—was a painstaking devotion to whatever job he had on hand. He was fitted to be a dependable, trustworthy country solicitor: probably he was meant to be nothing more than a managing clerk. But Mrs Hebb was bent on seeing him set up in practice for himself.

About the end of September 1899 Mrs Hebb came to see me at my office one night when I was working late there and she knew that I should be alone—I was at that time Mayor of Ullathwaite, and was so much occupied with my mayoral and magisterial duties that I had to leave my own professional business in the hands of Hebb and could only get to my office for supervising work in the evenings of days spent at the Town Hall. Mrs Hebb's visit was a surprise to me. But she soon let me know what she had come for and why she had come when she knew that I should be alone.

'Mr Radford,' she said, 'I called to-night because I knew you were often to be found at the office of an evening nowadays, and because I don't want my husband to know that I've been here. It's his night at the School Board meeting, and he never gets home from that before eleven o'clock, so I took advantage of his absence to come. I'm sure you'll excuse me when I tell you why I came.'

'Certainly, certainly, Mrs Hebb,' I said, reassuringly. 'Nothing wrong, I hope?'

'Oh, dear me, no, thank you, Mr Radford,' she replied. 'No—I just wanted to ask your advice, and, perhaps, your kind assistance. You see, Mr Radford, I want to do something for my husband.'

'Oh!' I said. 'I—I see. And what is it, Mrs Hebb?'

'Well, Mr Radford,' she continued, 'it's just this—neither I nor my family want Hebb to remain merely what he is—a managing clerk. We want him to rise in the world.'

'Very laudable ambition, Mrs Hebb,' I replied. 'And—Hebb? What does he want?'

'Hebb,' she answered, 'has not the ambition that I have: I mean, that I have for him. He's very well satisfied to be your right-hand man. But I—and my family—want him to be a principal. And lately, Mr Radford, I've persuaded him to write about two or three likely partnerships, and this week we've heard of one that in my opinion would just suit him—it's at Bridgwater, in the west of England, and near my old home——'

'So,' said I, with a laugh, 'it would suit you!'

'It would certainly be nice to be near one's own people,' she admitted. 'But there are other advantages. It's a partnership in a good old-fashioned, well-established firm, Mr Radford—Chauncey, Pugh, & Ledman. Chauncey's dead, and Pugh's dead, but——'

'But their names live after them,' I said. 'Well, and what else, Mrs Hebb? I suppose Hebb would have to find some money?'

'He would, Mr Radford,' she asserted, 'and that's just why he says he'll have no more to do with it, because he hasn't got the money. But, Mr Radford, I can find the money—at least, the greater part of it. Unknown to Hebb, I've been seeing what I could do. They want two thousand pounds. Well, my father's promised to find a thousand pounds at once, and I have five hundred of my very own——'

'Fifteen hundred, Mrs Hebb,' I said, having by this time a pretty good guess at what she had come for. 'Well, there's still five hundred to be raised. What about that?'

'Well, Mr Radford,' she answered, frankly. 'I thought perhaps you'd lend it. Not to Hebb—but to me. You can take my word for it that I'd see you were paid back—and in no long time, either.'

'I'm quite sure you'd do whatever you promised, Mrs Hebb,' I replied. 'And I'm not indisposed to help. But we must go into details. I suppose you've some correspondence with these people and with your father?'

That was how Mrs Hebb and I began to have business dealings, and to see each other occasionally. She was anxious to keep the affair and the arrangements secret from Hebb until everything was settled; consequently, Hebb did not know that I was going to see her at their cottage near Hagsdene Wood nor that she called on me once or twice at my office. And so matters stood on the 17th October—a fateful date, as things turned out.

Late in the evening of that 17th October I went to Hebb's cottage, where I knew I should find Mrs Hebb alone, that being the night when Hebb attended the meeting of a School Board at a place some little distance away from Ullathwaite. My definite object in calling was to return to Mrs Hebb certain documents and papers—correspondence with her father and with Mr Ledman—and to hand her a cheque for £500, which sum completed the £2000 necessary for the purchase of the partnership. I did not, of course, mention my destination on leaving my house: my wife and daughter doubtless believed that I was going to my office; as for my son, Richard, I believed him to be on his way to Lowsthorpe, some thirty miles away, on a visit to our friend Mr Verrill, a gentleman-farmer. I left the house in the ordinary course—but I may mention here that as I passed through the front hall I picked out, at random, a walking-stick, an ordinary, cheap oak stick, from among a miscellaneous collection of such things which stood in a rack near the front door.

It was about half-past nine when I called on Mrs Hebb: my business with her occupied nearly three quarters of an hour. I left her about—as near as I can reckon—ten minutes past ten. I had just reached her garden-gate when I heard steps coming through the wood: there was a path there which transected the wood from east to west. Not caring to be seen by whoever it was, I drew back into the shrubbery of some tall laurel bushes. There was a strong light shining through the transom above the front door of Hebb's cottage, and its rays fell full on the woodland path in front of the gate. The next instant there came into view on that path my son Richard, whom I had believed to be thirty miles away.

For the moment I fancied that Richard was making for Hebb's cottage. But when he was within half a dozen yards of its gate he swerved on a path that ran alongside their garden-hedge to certain meadows that sloped down to the valley, and within another minute or two the sound of his footsteps had ceased. In the momentary glimpse I had had of him I had noticed that he carried a parcel under one arm and swung a stick in the other hand. He was humming a tune as he passed out of my sight.

I attached no importance to the fact of seeing Dick there. I thought he had changed his mind about going to Lowsthorpe. I also thought that the reason of his being there, near Hebb's cottage, was that he was on his way to call on somebody—I made no guess at particulars—at one or other of the houses on the other side of the valley. After he had disappeared I left the shelter of the laurel bushes and the garden and, striking into the path which led to the town, I pulled out—or, rather, felt for—my cigar-case. Then I discovered that I had left it, and my walking-stick, on the table of Mrs Hebb's parlour. So

I returned to the cottage.

Being back there, I remained a little time longer, perhaps twenty minutes, rediscussing matters and arrangements with Mrs Hebb. I distinctly remember that the hands of her clock pointed to twenty-five minutes to eleven when I finally left the parlour. Smoking the cigar which I had just lighted, I set out along the path towards Ullathwaite. I had reached a point somewhere about fifty yards from the garden-gate when a man's figure suddenly started from behind the undergrowth and barred my progress. The light I have previously mentioned shone straight down that path, and it was sufficiently strong to show me that the man was Roger Maidment.

II

I cannot remember that I had ever had any business dealings with Maidment, but I knew him well enough by sight as a young man who had set up for himself in Ullathwaite as an accountant and rent-collector. Of course he knew me; as Mayor of Ullathwaite and a leading solicitor, I was known to everybody. And I was not surprised when he accosted me.

'Good evening, Mr Mayor!' he said. 'Nice evening.'

Good evening,' I replied. 'Very nice, as you say.'

I wanted to pass on, and wondered why he stood there, right in my way. I made as if to pass him, but he deliberately planted himself in front of me. And now he laughed, quietly, and there was a note in his laughter which I did not like the sound of.

'Fond of this part of the wood, Mr Mayor, aren't you?' he went on. 'Find it attractive, what?'

I drew back a pace, staring at him. But I saw that he was not drunk.

'Your remarks are offensive, sir!' I said, sharply. 'So is your manner! Allow me to pass!'

Again he barred the way—the path was a very narrow one—and again he laughed. And this time his laughter was both sneering and sinister.

'Not till we've had a word or two, Mr Mayor,' he said. 'This is a nice, quiet place for a bit of private talk. I said—you're fond of this quarter of the globe—so to speak. Has its attractions, eh?'

Again I stared at him. And after staring at him I made another attempt to pass—with the same result. Then I drew back still farther.

'I don't know what you mean, sir!' I said angrily. 'But you'll have to account for your strange conduct. Stand aside at once!'

He laughed once more—still more sneeringly.

'When I please!' he retorted. 'The whip's in my hands, Mr Mayor! What do I mean, eh? Well, if you want to know, I mean that Mrs Hebb is a very pretty woman. That's what I mean, Mr Mayor—just that!'

I saw then what he was after. Blackmail! And my temper rose.

'You infernal scoundrel!' I burst out. 'Do you dare——?'

'Keep calm, Mr Mayor, keep calm!' he interrupted, teasingly. 'No use going into tantrums, you know. I know a good deal more than you think. I've been keeping an eye on you. You've been visiting the pretty and charming Mrs Hebb when you and she knew you were safe from interruption or disturbance—on nights when Hebb was away: I've made a careful note of the dates. A nice little story for the inhabitants of Ullathwaite, Mr Radford! His Worship the Mayor—such a precise, proper, prunes-and-prisms gentleman!—philandering with a young married woman not half his age. How would you like me to tell it, Mr Radford? And would you like it plain or coloured? I can colour it a bit, you know. Or would you like to have it suppressed, kept secret? First edition destroyed before any publication, eh? In that case——'

I scarcely know how the thing happened: by that time I was almost beside myself with foolish, unreasoning anger. I had the heavy oak stick in my hand, and I dimly remember striking out at him, once, twice; the blows must have fallen on him so swiftly and suddenly that he hadn't time to lift his arm. And the next thing was that he was lying across the path at my feet, and in another moment I realized that I had killed him.

III

There have been several occasions in my life when I have had to make a quick decision, and to act on it as quickly as it was made. But I never realized the need of quick thought and immediate action as much as when I saw Maidment lying dead at my feet. And within a minute or two I knew what I must do, and was doing it. *Nobody must ever know how or why Maidment met his death!*—I must so contrive things that it must be thought that he had been waylaid and robbed of the money he had collected that night from the tenants of Hagsdene Park.

Maidment had gone down without as much as a cry—I must have struck him with more force than I had known. I stood for a second or two, listening, and heard nothing from any direction. Then I set to work. I took from his pockets all the money I could find—paper, coins—and thrust it into one of my own pockets. That done, I picked up the stick and went away. But before I had gone many yards I came alongside a rabbit-warren in the side of a sandy bank, which I had noticed once or twice in passing through the wood, and, acting on a sudden impulse, I thrust the stick into one of the burrows, pushing it inside as far as I could reach. It seemed to me a million to one that it should ever be disinterred from this hiding-place.

And then I went out of the wood. But not home—I was not equal to that. I was still quivering with anger and fury—at Maidment. I do not remember that I felt any regret at his death—I was thinking of him as a vile reptile whom I had been—unfortunately for myself—obliged to crush out of existence. All my concern was to shield myself and Mrs Hebb—but principally, I am bound to say, myself. I had my position, as Mayor of Ullathwaite and a leading man in the town, to think of: I also had my family to think of. I cursed Maidment in my heart for occasioning me this annoyance, but I considered him well served for his abominable attempt to blackmail me. And I did not intend that it should be found out that I had punished him with the loss of his life for that attempt.

I went away from the wood to my office in the town. There was nothing unusual in that. During my Mayoralty I often went to the office at night to work off arrears in my own business. It was very late, of course, when I let myself in, but the caretaker and his wife were still up. I got some fresh water, and, taking out a bottle of whisky which I kept in a cupboard in my private room, I took a stiff drink, followed by another.

Now, secure from interruption, I looked at what I had taken from Maidment's pockets. There were some cheques, some banknotes, some gold. I made a note of the total—about £112. Then I burned the cheques and the banknotes in the grate in my room, carefully noting that every scrap was consumed. But the gold—a few sovereigns—I carried into the clerks' room and threw it, without a glance at it, into a drawer in which we kept ready cash for office purposes. I hadn't the remotest idea that among the coins thus carelessly thrown aside there was one which could be identified.

IV

I heard of the death of Maidment during the course of the following morning. Hebb told me of it. Just as I had expected, the prevalent opinion was that Maidment had been waylaid, murdered, and robbed by somebody who knew that he collected rents at Hagsdene Park on the evening of the 17th of each month.

I went about my usual avocations that morning, feeling sure that all was safe. I could not see how the so-called murder of Maidment could be traced to anyone. The cheques and notes were already nonexistent; nobody could tell one sovereign from another. It seemed to me an utter impossibility that the police should get any clue, or should ever be able to find out at whose hand Maidment met his—in my opinion, justly deserved—fate.

But soon after noon that day, the 18th October, I received a rude shock. The Superintendent of Police for the County, Henderson, called on me at the Mayor's Parlour, and told me that at half-past ten o'clock that morning my son Richard, in discharge of a betting debt, had paid to one Fardale, a bookmaker, the sum of fifty-one pounds, in notes and gold, and that among the gold was a marked—perforated—sovereign which had been positively identified as one paid the previous evening by a Mr Collingwood, of Hagsdene Park, to Maidment.

Now I knew at once what had happened. *Richard had taken some gold out of the drawer in our clerks' room that morning!* Among it had been the sovereign referred to. So—instead of suspicion falling on me fate had ordained that it should fall on my son!

Again I had to think quickly. And from the first I saw that Richard was safe. Why? *Because I knew that the banknotes paid to Maidment by the tenants of Hagsdene Park had been burned by my own hand!* Those handed by Richard to Fardale had not come from that source. As regarded the marked sovereign, that could be got over.

From the moment in which Henderson accused Richard in my presence, Richard took the right course. He announced his intention of preserving a strict silence. He would say nothing to anybody. Beyond an emphatic assurance to me and to his mother that he had neither murdered nor robbed Maidment he said no further word. Arrested, brought before the magistrates, and remanded; eventually committed to take his trial at the next Grandminster Assizes, he let things take their course. Not a word could be got out of him as to where he spent the night of October 17, nor where he obtained the bulk of the money with which to pay Fardale.

But between the time of Richard's arrest and his final appearance before the magistrates I had been thinking, and acting in secret in my thoughts. *Where was Richard going when I saw him pass Hebb's cottage?* Unknown to him or to anybody else, I had an idea. He was going to see Mrs Norrington, the young and pretty wife of an elderly, invalid husband, a rich man who lived in a big house in the valley beneath Hagsdene Wood. She and Richard had played together in an amateur dramatic performance the previous winter, and although he had never mentioned the matter to anyone I had had an idea that he had been dangling after her. And putting two and two together, I came to the conclusion that Mrs Norrington had found for him most of the money which he wanted for Fardale, and that he had made up the exact amount by taking some gold from the cash-box at the office. I also concluded that he had spent the night under the Norringtons' roof. Now, as I had seen him pass Hebb's cottage at about five minutes past ten, and as Maidment, according to the doctors, met his death not before half-past ten, and as Richard would reach the Norringtons' at a quarter past ten, it would be the simplest thing in the world to prove an alibi—if the worst came to the worst. *But only Mrs Norrington could prove it.*

But at this stage I was pulled up short. I discovered that Mrs Norrington was not at home on the night of the 17th October! She was, and had been for some little time, at Harrogate with her husband. On learning this, I went over to see her, and, after exerting some pressure, got the absolute truth out of her. Richard had been to see her on the evening of October 17, and had told her his predicament. She had a sum of forty-five pounds in banknotes in a drawer of her dressing-table; she gave him the key, and a key of the locked-up house: he returned to Ullathwaite and got the money . . . and, of course, stayed in the house all night.

So now everything was clear to me. I made Mrs Norrington swear that if it became absolutely necessary she would come forward and tell what she had told me. But I did not believe it ever would be necessary—still, I caused an anonymous letter to be forwarded from London to the presiding magistrates at Ullathwaite indicating what would be done under certain circumstances.

Those circumstances never arose. I never believed Richard to be in danger from the very first. I never expected that the jury would hesitate for one moment—indeed, I was amazed when they left the box to consider their verdict. I was still more amazed when several hours elapsed and they were still considering it. I have never known how or why it was that they were so dilatory—there must have been some very stupid persons among them. But the verdict came at last—*Not Guilty!*

From that moment until now I have dismissed the Maidment affair from my mind. My great object in life has been to recompense my son Richard for any anxiety, trouble, pain he was put to during that unfortunate episode. He will read this when I am gone, and I trust he will understand.

(*signed*) JOHN RADFORD

That is the whole of what my father wrote. I understand it . . . and I have nothing more to say.

Printed in Great Britain
by Amazon

47107014R00088